Welcome to the world of
St Piran's Hospital

Next to the rugged shores of Penhally Bay
lies the picturesque Cornish town of St Piran,
where you'll find a bustling hospital famed
for the dedication, talent and passion
of its staff—on and off the wards!

Under the warmth of the Cornish sun
Italian doctors, heart surgeons, and
playboy princes discover that romance
blossoms in the most unlikely of places…

You'll also meet the devilishly handsome
Dr Josh O'Hara and the beautiful,
fragile Megan Phillips…and discover the
secret that tore these star-crossed lovers apart.

Turn the page to step into St Piran's—
where every drama has a dreamy doctor…
and a happy ending.

Dear Reader

Having taken part in the *Penhally* series, I was honoured to be part of this exciting new project, returning to Cornwall but broadening the focus and scope beyond the village of Penhally itself. This new series centres around St Piran's Hospital and its staff, delving into their lives and their loves. I am delighted to bring you ST PIRAN'S: ITALIAN SURGEON, FORBIDDEN BRIDE.

Consultant neurosurgeon Giovanni Correzi has been through dark times, and now focuses on his patients and his charity work. Highly respected and sought-after, why has he left a high-flying post in London and moved to rural Cornwall? Gio has strong reasons for choosing St Piran's. He just didn't expect to meet a woman who awakens his heart from its long hibernation. Four years ago, counsellor Jessica Carmichael's world came crashing down around her. She has reinvented herself and carved her own niche in Cornwall, but a dark shadow hangs over her, setting her apart and holding her back from life.

Gio and Jess share an immediate but unwanted attraction. Their professional respect rapidly grows into a close friendship, and when events cause them to spend time together it becomes increasingly difficult for them to deny their feelings. But Jess is adamant that friendship is all they can share, and Gio has to tread gently to learn her secrets, earn her trust and win her heart.

Can these two come together with a promise of new hope for the future and the second chance at love they both deserve? Gio and Jess touched my heart. I hope you will share their journey and fall in love with them too! Welcome to St Piran's!

Love

Margaret

www.margaretmcdonagh.com
margaret.mcdonagh@yahoo.co.uk

ST PIRAN'S:
ITALIAN SURGEON,
FORBIDDEN BRIDE

BY
MARGARET McDONAGH

Falkirk Council	
GM	
Askews & Holts	
AF	£13.99

MILLS & BOON

First published in Great Britain 2011
by Mills & Boon,
an imprint of Harlequin (UK) Limited,
Large Print edition 2011
Eton House, 18-24 Paradise Road,
Richmond, Surrey TW9 1SR

© Harlequin Books S.A. 2011

Special thanks and acknowledgement are given
to Margaret McDonagh for her contribution to the
St Piran's Hospital series

ISBN: 978 0 263 21750 6

Printed and bound in Great Britain
by CPI Antony Rowe, Chippenham, Wiltshire

Margaret McDonagh says of herself: 'I began losing myself in the magical world of books from a very young age, and I always knew that I had to write, pursuing the dream for over twenty years, often with cussed stubbornness in the face of rejection letters! Despite having numerous romance novellas, short stories and serials published, the news that my first "proper book" had been accepted by Harlequin Mills & Boon for their Medical™ Romance line brought indescribable joy! Having a passion for learning makes researching an involving pleasure, and I love developing new characters, getting to know them, setting them challenges to overcome. The hardest part is saying goodbye to them, because they become so real to me. And I always fall in love with my heroes! Writing and reading books, keeping in touch with friends, watching sport and meeting the demands of my four-legged companions keeps me well occupied. I hope you enjoy reading this book as much as I loved writing it.'

www.margaretmcdonagh.com
margaret.mcdonagh@yahoo.co.uk

With special thanks to:

The Medical™ Romance team, for inviting me to be a part of this wonderful project, and my fellow authors for their support. Especially…
Jo, Lucy, Mimi, Sheila, Carol, Caroline,
Kate and Maggie

Charlie & Will—for 'Charlie'…
and for making the best bears in the world!

Namlife for the information on living with HIV:
www.namlife.org

ST PIRAN'S HOSPITAL
*Where every drama has a dreamy doctor...
and a happy ending.*

Last month we brought you the first two St Piran's stories!

**Nick Tremayne and Kate Althorp
finally got their happy-ever-after in:**
ST PIRAN'S: THE WEDDING OF THE YEAR
by Caroline Anderson

**Dr Izzy Bailey was swept off her feet
by sexy Spaniard Diego Ramirez**
ST PIRAN'S: RESCUING PREGNANT CINDERELLA
by Carol Marinelli

*And there's plenty more romance
brewing in St Piran's!*

**The arrival of Italian neurosurgeon Giovanni Corezzi
will make your heart beat faster this month**
ST PIRAN'S: ITALIAN SURGEON, FORBIDDEN BRIDE
by Margaret McDonagh

**The following month, daredevil doc William MacNeil
unexpectedly discovers that he's a father**
ST PIRAN'S: DAREDEVIL, DOCTOR...AND DAD!
by Anne Fraser

Then the new heart surgeon has everyone's pulses racing
ST PIRAN'S: THE BROODING HEART SURGEON
by Alison Roberts

**Fireman Tom Nicholson steals Flora Loveday's heart
the month after**
ST PIRAN'S: THE FIREMAN AND NURSE LOVEDAY
by Kate Hardy

**Then newborn twins could just bring a marriage miracle
for Brianna and Connor Taylor**
ST PIRAN'S: TINY MIRACLE TWINS
by Maggie Kingsley

**And finally playboy Prince Alessandro Cavalieri
comes to St Piran**
ST PIRAN'S: PRINCE ON THE CHILDREN'S WARD
by Sarah Morgan

CHAPTER ONE

'You need Jessica Carmichael.'

He didn't *need* anyone...not any more.

Giovanni Corezzi bit back his instant denial of the suggestion made by paediatric registrar Dr Megan Phillips. It was his first day as consultant neurosurgeon at St Piran's Hospital in Cornwall and although his primary focus was always on doing his best for his patients, he also hoped to make a good impression and to form a friendly working relationship with his new colleagues.

'Jessica Carmichael?'

He frowned, disturbed at the way the unknown woman's name flowed from his tongue. As if it were a caress. And somehow important. What nonsense was he thinking? With an impatient shake of his head, he refocused on Megan.

'Jess is a hospital counsellor. She's very knowledgeable and good with patients and their relatives,' the paediatric registrar explained with obvious admiration. 'Unfortunately we don't have extra time for everyone. Jess fills that gap.'

'I'll bear it in mind,' Gio replied, knowing the involvement of a counsellor was often helpful to his patients but reluctant to bring one in now.

'It's your decision.' Megan's disappointment and disagreement were apparent. 'I think you'd find Jess useful in Cody Rowland's case.'

Gio bit back irritation as the young registrar questioned his judgement. Instead of an instant retort, however, he considered whether he had missed anything regarding the young boy admitted to his care. Three-year-old Cody had fallen from a climbing frame two weeks previously, but had not shown any symptoms at the time. Recently he had become increasingly listless, complaining of a headache, going off his food and feeling nauseous. His frightened parents had brought him to the hospital that morning.

A and E consultant Josh O'Hara had examined Cody and called the neurology team. Busy in Theatre, Gio had sent his registrar to do an assessment. The subsequent tests, including a

CT scan, had revealed the presence of a chronic subdural haematoma. As the bleed had continued and the clot had increased in size, it had caused a rise in pressure and the swelling brain to press on the skull, causing bruising and a restriction in blood flow.

Cody was now on the children's ward and awaiting surgery. Unless he carried out the operation soon, Gio feared the boy's condition would deteriorate and, if the clot and pressure continued to grow, there was a possibility of irreversible brain damage.

It was after noon and his first day was proving to be a hectic one. That morning he had undertaken three minor and routine operations—as minor and routine as any brain surgery procedures could be—and his first neurological clinic was scheduled later that afternoon. Before that, he needed to return to the operating theatre with Cody.

'I'm sure this woman is good at her job,' he commented, 'but Cody—'

'Cody might need Jess at some point. Right now I'm thinking of his parents.'

Gio hated to admit it, but she was right. He *did* have concerns about the Rowlands and that Megan had picked up on the same signs was something he should find pleasing, not irritating.

'They aren't coping well,' he conceded with frustration. 'And their anxiety is distressing Cody. I need him to be settled for surgery—and for his parents to be calm and understand why we need to operate. I wish to press on them the urgency without further panicking them. They are listening but not hearing, you know?'

'I know,' Megan agreed. 'They're in denial… Mrs Rowland particularly.'

'Exactly so. Which is understandable. I'm not unsympathetic but I don't know how much time we have to play with.'

Megan hesitated, as if unsure of her ground. 'That's why I suggested Jess. I'm sorry to keep on about her, and I'm not questioning your skills,' she added hastily as his eyebrows snapped together. 'But I know how helpful she is in these situations. Everyone in the hospital likes Jess. She's a wonderful listener…and it isn't just the patients and their relatives who benefit. The staff frequently offload their problems on her, too. She's definitely your woman.'

Gio's frown returned in earnest, both at Megan's phraseology and the implication of her words. 'I don't know…'

Was he being too hasty? It was uncharacteristic of him not to listen to the suggestions of others, even if they were his juniors. He considered his reluctance to follow Megan's advice. Was it because he didn't want his new colleagues to think he couldn't do his job? Here he was, halfway through his first day and already needing to call in someone else to help with a case! He shook his head. What mattered was the well-being of his patients, not his own status.

Checking his watch, aware that *he* was now the one wasting precious time, he wondered how long it would take for Ms Carmichael to arrive. Once she was there, he would need to bring her up to date on the case and, as yet, he had no idea how much she understood of medical issues.

'Won't she be tied up with existing appointments?' he asked Megan. 'Cody can't afford to wait much longer.'

'Jess doesn't work like that, Mr Corezzi. She's on call and responds to whichever department or ward has need of her. It's just a matter of paging her—she usually comes right away,' the paediatric registrar explained, jotting a note on the front of Cody's file.

'Call me Gio.' He made the invitation with a distracted smile as he considered his options. He needed Cody in Theatre without further delay. If this counsellor could help facilitate that, then so be it. 'All right, Megan, please call her,' he invited, decision made, adding a word of caution. 'However, if she's not here soon, we may have to move without her.'

Megan's smile was swift. 'You won't be sorry, Gio,' she assured him, and he could only hope she was right.

'I'll ensure the operating theatre and my team are ready. And I'll arrange for the anaesthetist to assess Cody,' he informed her. 'Everything will be in place and we can move quickly—*when* we have the Rowlands' consent.'

As Megan went to the ward office to organise the page, an inexplicable shiver of apprehension and anticipation rippled down Gio's spine. He had done the right thing for Cody. So why did he feel unsettled? And why did he have the disturbing notion that in bringing Jessica Carmichael on board he would be taking on much more than he had bargained for?

'Consultants don't spend time taking histories or chatting to patients and their relatives. That's why they have registrars and juniors,' Jess protested with a mix of wry cynicism and surprise.

Megan chuckled. 'This consultant does. He's pretty amazing, Jess, and very hands on.'

The news that Mr Corezzi remained on the ward was disturbing enough, but knowing Megan was so taken with their new consultant neurosurgeon left Jess feeling more unsettled. A sense of premonition refused to be banished. On edge, she opened her notebook and balanced it on top of the other items she carried, jotting down a few pointers as her friend gave a brief summation of Cody's case.

'Mr Corezzi…Gio…will give you more detail,' Megan added, the prospect making Jess feel more nervous.

'And Cody is three,' she mused, considering how best to help. 'I'll get Charlie.'

'Who is Charlie?'

The question came from behind her and the deep, throaty voice with its distinctive Italian accent not only identified its owner but set every nerve-ending tingling. Jess knew it was his first day there, and within moments of his arrival the overactive grapevine had been buzzing about the gorgeous new consultant. Female staff the length and breadth of the hospital had been preening themselves, eager to meet him and make an impression on him.

She had not been one of them.

Jess tensed, her knuckles whitening as her fingers tightened their grip on her files. Clutching them like a protective shield, and feeling suddenly scared in a way she didn't understand, she turned around and saw Giovanni Corezzi for the first time.

Oh, my!

For once the rumourmill had been right. The new Italian surgeon *was* something special to look at and even she, who had sworn off men a long time ago, could appreciate the view. A bit like window-shopping, she thought, smothering an inappropriate smile. You could admire the goods even though you had no intention of buying. But her inner humour vanished in the face of her body's impossible-to-ignore reaction.

She hated the breathless feeling that made it difficult to fill her lungs, the ache that knotted her stomach, the too-fast beat of her heart, and jelly-like knees that felt unable to support her. The instinctive responses were unnerving and unwanted. She had not been attracted to any man for a long time—had not expected or wished to be. Not since her life had taken an abrupt change of direction four years ago, turning her world upside down and having an irrevocable impact on her future, forcing her not only to abandon her hopes and dreams but to reinvent herself to survive. The Jess Carmichael of today was a very different person from the one then...one who could no longer indulge in many things, including uncharacteristic flights of fancy over a good-looking man, even if he did stir her blood in ways it had never been stirred before.

Trying to shrug off the disturbing feelings, she allowed herself a quick inspection of the imposing man who stood before her looking relaxed and at ease. His dark hair was short, thick and well groomed. In his early thirties, and topping six feet, he had an olive-toned complexion and the kind of chiselled jawline that would make him sought after in Hollywood or gracing the pages of fashion magazines. Not that he was fashionable at the moment, dressed as he was in hospital scrubs, suggesting he had come to the ward from the operating theatre.

The shapeless trousers and short-sleeved tunic should have been unflattering but they failed to mask the strength and lean athleticism of his body, while their colour emphasised the intense blueness of his eyes. Under straight, dark brows and fringed by long, dusky lashes, they were the shade of the rarest tanzanite. They regarded her with a wariness she shared, a suspicion that had her shifting uncomfortably, and the kind of masculine interest and sensual awareness that frightened her witless.

Aware that Megan was making the introductions, Jess struggled to pull herself together.

'Ms Carmichael.'

The throaty rumble of his voice made her pulse race and ruined her attempt at sang-froid. 'Hello, Mr Corezzi.'

Jess dragged her gaze free and focused on the leanly muscled forearms crossed over his broad chest. As he moved, she juggled the files and assorted items she carried around the hospital, anxious to avoid shaking hands. Instead, she fished out one of her cards, careful to ensure she didn't touch him. His fingers closed around the card and she couldn't help but notice that he had nice hands. Surgeon's hands...capable, cared for and with short, well-manicured nails. There was no wedding ring and no tell-tale sign to suggest he had recently worn one. His only accessory was the watch on his left wrist with its mesh strap and midnight-blue dial.

The sound of Megan's pager made Jess jump but the distraction helped cut the growing tension.

'I'm needed in A and E,' Megan told them with evident reluctance, her cheeks pale and lines of strain around her mouth.

'Are you OK?' Jess asked, knowing her friend's reluctance stemmed from some unexplained issues she had with Josh O'Hara, the charismatic consultant who had joined St Piran's trauma team in the spring.

'I'll be fine.'

The words lacked conviction and Jess was concerned. Tall and slender, Megan appeared delicate, but although she possessed an inner strength, she had seemed more fragile than usual these last few weeks. Instinct made Jess want to give her friend a hug, but she hung back, keeping the physical distance she had maintained between herself and everyone else these last four years.

'I'm here if you need me,' she offered instead, conscious of the disturbing nearness of Giovanni Corezzi, whose presence prevented her saying more.

'Thanks.' Megan squared her shoulders, determination mixing with anxiety and inner hurt that shadowed her green eyes. 'I'll see you later. Good luck with the Rowlands. And Cody's surgery.'

Alone with Giovanni Corezzi, Jess felt a return of the tension and awareness that surged between them. Determined to focus on work, and needing to put distance between herself and the disturbing new surgeon, Jess murmured an apology and escaped to the ward office to track down Charlie.

Gio released a shaky breath as the surprising Jessica Carmichael walked away. He had no idea who Charlie was, or how he was relevant to the current problem, but he had greater things to worry about. Namely Jessica and his unaccountably disturbing reaction to her.

As the staff went about their work on the busy ward, he leaned against the wall and pressed one hand to his stomach. The moment he'd seen Jessica, it had felt as if he'd been sat on by an elephant. She was younger than he'd expected, perhaps in her late twenties. Below average height, she looked smart but casual, dressed for the August heat in a multi-coloured crinkle-cotton skirt that fell to her knees and a short-sleeved green shirt, her hospital ID clipped, like his own, to the top pocket.

Her eyes were a captivating and unusual olive green, while her hair—a gift from mother nature—was a vibrant auburn, with shades from burnished chestnut, like a conker fresh from its casing, to rich copper red. The luxuriant waves were confined in a thick plait which bobbed between her shoulder blades. He longed to see it unrestrained and to run his fingers through its glory.

When Jessica emerged from the ward office, the disturbing heaviness pressed on him once more. He straightened, shocked by the slam of attraction that shot through him. The cut of her shirt highlighted firm, full breasts, while the sway of her skirt hinted at curvy hips and thighs. He found her rounded, feminine figure so much more appealing than the reed-thin bodies many women aspired to.

Gio took an involuntary step back, disturbed by the surge of desire that threatened to overwhelm him with its unexpected intensity. This was the first time he had even *noticed* a woman for a long time. He couldn't believe it had been five years— No! He slammed his brain shut on *those* thoughts. This was neither the time nor the place. But he'd allowed a crack in the internal armour encasing the memories, the pain and his heart, and panic swelled within him. He didn't want to be attracted to anyone, yet he could not deny the strength of his reaction to Jessica or the way his body was reawakening and making new desires and needs known.

Disconcerted, he met her gaze and saw her eyes widen in shock at the unmasked emotions she read in his. She kept a safe gap between them, but she was close enough for him to see her shock turn to confusion, followed by answering knowledge and then alarm. Silence stretched and the air crackled with electricity. It was clear Jessica didn't want the attraction any more than he did, but that didn't make it go away. And, perversely, her reluctance intrigued him and made him want to learn more about her.

She stepped aside to allow a nurse pushing a wheelchair to pass, her smile transforming her pretty face and trapping the air in his lungs. Cross with himself, he was about to return to the business of Cody Rowland when she shifted the things she was carrying and he noticed the teddy-bear puppet she wore on one hand.

'Meet Charlie,' she invited, holding up the plush toy, which had marbled brown fur and a friendly, mischievous face, its mouth open as if laughing. 'He helps break the ice and explain things to young children, calming their fears.'

The husky but melodic burr of her soft Scottish accent was sensual and set his heart thudding. Feeling as flustered as a teenager with his first crush, he struggled to ignore his unwanted reaction and focus on the matter at hand.

'Very clever.' Her innovative method impressed him. He reached out and gently shook the teddy bear by the paw. 'It's nice to meet you, Charlie.'

Jessica's flustered reaction confirmed his suspicion that giving him her card had been a ruse to avoid shaking hands. Was it him, or did she dislike touching other people, too? That he was immediately attuned to her unsettled him further.

'What are the priorities with Cody?' Jessica asked, moving them onto ground which, he felt sure, made her feel more comfortable. 'Have his parents signed the consent form?'

'Not yet.' Gio ran the fingers of one hand through his hair in frustration. 'The injury occurred over two weeks ago,' he explained, unsure how much Megan had told her. 'The parents are too upset to understand that while Cody may have appeared fine at first, the situation has changed.'

'And you don't want to waste more time.'

Grateful that Jessica was on his wavelength, Gio smiled. 'Exactly so.'

'He's deteriorating more quickly?' she asked, glancing at the notes.

'What was a slow bleed building a chronic subdural haematoma could be worsening,' he outlined, sharing his concerns. 'Or something more serious could be underlying it.'

Jessica nodded, making her beautiful hair gleam. 'And the longer you wait, the more chance there is of permanent brain damage.'

'I'm afraid so.'

'His parents must be very confused.' Her expression softened with understanding. 'They may feel guilty for not realising that what seemed an innocuous incident has become something so serious.'

'There is no question of blame, although such feelings are common,' he agreed, impressed by Jessica.

Her smile was rueful. 'I come across this in a wide variety of circumstances. We need to explain things to the Rowlands without frightening them further.'

'Yes…and Megan says you're the best person to help.'

A wash of colour warmed her flawless alabaster cheeks. 'I'll do what I can, of course.'

'Thank you, Jessica.'

Again her name felt right, unsettling him and curbing his amusement at her flustered reaction. Ignoring the hum of attraction between them by concentrating on work might not be effective long term, but hopefully it would get them through this encounter.

'Do you have suggestions about the Rowlands?'

Her relief was evident and she nodded again, loosening some strands of fiery hair, which tumbled around her face. As she raised her free hand, he saw that her fingers were ring free, and that she wore a narrow silver-toned watch around her wrist. She tucked the errant curls behind her ear, drawing his attention to the attractive stud earrings she wore. Set in white metal, the olive green stones matched her eyes and he made a mental note to discover the identity of the gem that so suited her.

'We need their consent so Cody can go to Theatre without delay. Then I can spend time with them and run through everything in more detail.' Even, white teeth nibbled the sensual swell of her rosy lower lip, nearly giving him heart failure. 'Do you have a rough guestimate on how long the operation might take?' she queried, snapping his attention back to business. 'The Rowlands will ask—and I need to re-organise my schedule to support them.'

Gio was encouraged by Jessica's common-sense

approach, knowledge and apparent dedication to her patients. With real hope of a resolution, he gave her all the information he could.

'Can you talk with the father while I try the mother?' she asked next, walking briskly towards Cody's room.

He would happily do anything to speed things along. 'No problem.'

Following her, he admired her gently rounded, mouth-watering curves. As she stepped into Cody's room, sunlight spilling through the window made the natural red, copper and chestnut tones of her hair glow like living flames, captivating him. And, for the briefest instant, as he stood close behind her before she shifted to give him more room, he could have sworn he caught a faint, tantalising aroma of chocolate.

Fanciful notions vanished as he observed that Cody appeared more listless than when he had checked him several minutes ago. His frightened young mother sat close to him, clinging to his hand, tears spilling down her cheeks. The father, scarcely more than a boy himself, stood to one side, pale and withdrawn, at a loss to know what to do.

Jessica glanced over her shoulder and he met her gaze. The connection between them felt electric and intense, and it took a huge effort to look away. Clearing his throat, he introduced her to the Rowlands.

As Jessica began the delicate process of winning the trust of the troubled young family, Gio released another shaky breath. He was in big trouble. He had sensed Jessica would be more than he'd bargained for. Professionally. What he could never have foreseen was the impact she would have on him personally. It was unexpected, unwanted and scary. But bubbling within, as yet unacknowledged and unexplored, was growing excitement.

Even as they worked together to see Cody and his parents through the trauma that had befallen them, Gio was aware of the simmering connection between himself and Jessica. However hard they fought it, it was not going away.

All he knew for sure was that Jessica threatened

to blow the ordered and lonely world he had lived in these last five years wide apart, and that her impact on his life would not leave him unscathed.

CHAPTER TWO

SHE didn't *look* any different.

Jess peered at her reflection in the mirror above the basin in the tiny bathroom next to her office. She wasn't sure what she'd expected to see, but she *felt* different. Changed somehow. And scared. Because of Giovanni Corezzi. Thinking about him made her pulse race and raised her temperature to an uncomfortable level—one she couldn't blame on the scorching August weather.

After splashing cool water on her overheated cheeks, she buried her face in the softness of her towel. Even with her eyes closed, images of St Piran's new Italian surgeon filled her mind. Unsettled by her reaction to him, she had endeavoured to keep things on a professional footing, determined to banish the disturbing feelings he roused within her.

She hadn't wanted to like him, but it had proved

impossible not to. Ignoring the inexplicable and overwhelming blaze of attraction would have been easier had he been arrogant and horrible to work with, but nothing was further from the truth. He'd been compassionate and patient. As his initial suspicion had evaporated once he had witnessed her with the Rowlands, the likelihood was that she would be called to work with him again.

What was she going to do?

Jess sighed, discarding the towel and glancing at her reflection again. Less than an hour in his company had left her shaken and anxious. Megan had been right to describe him as hands on and caring. It was something Jess admired, yet it made him even more dangerous to her.

She had to find a way to limit his impact on her. He had reawakened things long forgotten, things she would sooner remained buried. She had to fight the desire he roused in her...because nothing could come of it. *Ever.* And she was leaving herself open to heartache if, even for a moment, she allowed herself to imagine anything else.

For the last four years, since the bombshell had hit her, changing her life for ever, she had turned in on herself, keeping focused on her new career and keeping people at bay. She hadn't worked so hard to reinvent herself to allow the first man to stir her long-dormant hormones into action to undo everything she had achieved. In the un-likely event she could ever trust a man again, there was no way she could allow any kind of relationship to develop. Not beyond friendship. To do so would be too great a risk. Besides, once Giovanni learned the truth she had kept secret for so long, he wouldn't want her anyway.

Quashing disobedient feelings of disappoint-ment and regret—and, worse, a flash of self-pity—Jess hardened her battered heart. She had to keep Giovanni Corezzi at a distance and ensure any meetings with him were kept as pro-fessional and brief as possible.

Shocked how late it was, she returned to her office. She'd had to rearrange her schedule for the Rowlands, which meant she had much to catch up on and now she would have to rush if she was not to be late for an important appointment.

Five days ago, and less than three weeks after moving into the run-down cottage she had bought near Penhally village, an unseasonal storm had caused serious damage. Today the insurance company's assessor was carrying out an inspection, after which Jess hoped permission would be given for the repairs. The sooner the better... before anyone discovered the unconventional lengths she was going to to keep a roof over her head.

Smothering her guilt, she took care of a few urgent tasks before shutting down her computer. She just had time to dash across the grounds to see hospital handyman Sid Evans and collect the precious cargo he was watching for her.

'Hello, Jess, love,' the kindly man greeted her as she hurried through his open workshop door. 'Everything is ready for you.'

'Thanks, Sid.'

'Here we are, all present and correct,' he told her in his lilting Welsh accent as he handed her a basket.

'I'm sorry to rush, Sid. Thanks for your help.'

'No worries.' He smiled, but Jess could see

the sadness that lurked in his eyes. Following the recent death of Winnie, Sid's beloved wife of forty years, Jess had taken time to visit with him. 'And I'm the one who's grateful. You've been wonderful, love, letting me talk about my Winnie. I'll not forget it.'

'It's been my privilege,' she replied, a lump in her throat.

Jess hurried back to the psychology unit, glad everyone had left for the day, allowing her to sneak the basket into her odd little annexe at the back of the building. Dubbed the 'cubby hole', it had been assigned to her as the only spare room available, but she couldn't have been more pleased. Apart from the office and next-door bathroom, it had an adjoining anteroom and a basic kitchen. Away from the main offices, it gave her privacy, which suited her just fine. Especially with circumstances as they were… circumstances no one else knew about and which brought another surge of guilt.

Setting down the basket, Jess checked the contents then picked up her bag and keys. The sooner she went home, the sooner she could return to

St Piran's. Hopefully she would be too busy in the coming hours to think about Giovanni Corezzi.

Opening her office door, she hurried out, only to collide with something solid and warm and smelling divinely of clean male with a hint of citrus and musk. Her 'Oh' of surprise was muffled against a broad chest as she lost her balance.

'Easy there,' Giovanni's voice soothed.

His hands steadied her, closing on her bare arms above the elbows. She felt the impact of his touch in every particle of her being, the brush of his fingers on sensitive skin making her tingle. She felt as if she'd been branded. A bolt of awareness and long-suppressed need blazed through her, scaring her.

The urge to lean into him and savour the moment was very strong. It seemed for ever since she had been touched and held, even in a platonic way. Not that there was anything *platonic* about the way Giovanni made her feel! But that knowledge acted like a bucket of icy water. Panic gripped her, both at the physical contact and her overwhelming reaction to this man. The need to break the spell overrode every-thing else and she struggled free, her desperation causing her to push away from him with more force than she had intended.

'What are you doing here?' she challenged brusquely.

Intense blue eyes regarded her with curiosity. 'Forgive me, I didn't know this part of the hospital was out of bounds.' His tone was gently teasing, but a blush stained her cheeks in acknowledge-ment of her uncharacteristic rudeness.

'It's not, of course, Mr Corezzi, but—' Jess broke off. Everything about him threw her into confusion.

'Please, call me Gio. I came to update you on Cody,' he explained, his throaty voice and sexy accent sending a shiver down her spine. 'And to thank you for your help.'

Her breath locked in her lungs as he rewarded her with a full-wattage smile. 'I was just doing my job.'

'I also wish to discuss another patient soon to

be admitted whom I feel will benefit from your involvement,' he continued.

'That's fine. But is it urgent? I'm in a hurry.'

Although she had softened her tone, his dark eyebrows drew together in a frown. 'It's not urgent, but I hoped you'd have a minute…'

'I'm afraid I don't.' Jess cursed her stiltedness. She seemed unable to behave normally around him. 'I'm sorry, I have to rush home. I'll talk with you later.'

Eager to make her escape without him seeing inside her office and discovering the secret she had kept hidden so far, Jess fumbled behind her for the handle and pulled the door closed with a determined snap. She turned round, removing herself from his inspection, locked her office and pocketed the key. Then, carefully skirting him, she walked briskly to the main entrance, conscious of him following her.

'Jessica…'

The way he said her name tied her insides into knots. It wasn't just his voice or pronunciation but that he alone used her full name and made it sound like a caress. Thankful she had a genuine excuse to escape, she opened the front door and stepped aside for him to exit ahead of her.

'I have to run,' she said, concerned at his reluctance to leave.

A muscle pulsed along the masculine line of his jaw, indicating his dissatisfaction. When he stepped outside, allowing her to do the same, the door swinging closed and the lock clicking into place, Jess released the breath she hadn't realised she'd been holding.

He looked down at her, a brooding expression on his far-too-handsome face. 'Later.'

It was more demand than question and it filled Jess with alarm...and a dangerous sense of excited anticipation that was the most scary of all.

'Later,' she allowed reluctantly.

As she hurried towards her car, she sensed him watching her. So much for her earlier resolution. He was going to be more difficult to avoid than she'd anticipated. And this second encounter had confirmed what a risk he posed to the carefully constructed world she had manufactured for herself. Now a sexy Italian neurosurgeon had bulldozed his way into her life and was in danger of unravelling everything she had worked so hard for.

Heavy-hearted at the way his first day at St Piran's was ending, Gio washed, disposed of his scrubs and dressed in the jeans and short-sleeved shirt he had pulled on after arriving home. He'd not long left the hospital after making a final check of his patients when the emergency call had come for him to return.

A multidisciplinary team had assembled in Theatre, but despite their best efforts their nineteen-year-old casualty had succumbed to severe chest trauma and brain damage after an alcohol-induced accident.

Gio sighed at the waste of a life. Pain stabbed inside him as his thoughts strayed to another young life that had been cut cruelly short and he closed his eyes, determined to control his emotions and push the destructive memories away. Instead, he found himself thinking of Jessica Carmichael.

His impulsive visit to her office in the psychology

unit—situated in one of the buildings adjacent to the main hospital and abutting the consultants' car park—had not gone to plan. He usually got on well with people. *'You could sell sand in the desert, Cori!'* Remembering the teasing words brought both amusement and an ache to his heart. Friendliness, politeness and a touch of flattery soothed troubled waters, but it wasn't working with Jessica, who remained tense and reserved.

Their unsatisfactory encounter had disappointed and confused him. He lived for his job, trying each day to make up for the failings that had haunted him for the last five years. Which was why his immediate and intense response to Jessica had shocked him. She had affected him on a deeply personal level. And he didn't *do* personal. Not any more. His reaction—and the attraction he wished he could deny—left him disconcerted and off balance.

When she had rushed out of her office and cannoned into him, instinct had taken over and he'd caught her as she'd stumbled. He'd felt the incredible softness of her skin under his fingers, the press of her femininely curved body against him, and he'd breathed in the teasing aroma of chocolate that lingered on her hair and skin. His attraction and body's response to her had been instant and undeniable.

But it was Jessica's reactions that had left him puzzled and unsettled. Her alarm had been real, and he had not imagined the panic in her beautiful green eyes as she'd wrenched herself free. For some reason Jessica didn't like to touch or be touched and he was determined to find out what lay behind it. There were several possibilities and each one caused him concern.

Gio stepped out of the surgeons' wash room, unsure what to do next. Why had Jessica been so dismissive of him and in such a rush to leave? He was positive she had felt the same bolt of awareness that had slammed into him when they'd first met. And that it had scared her. So could it be, he wondered, heading to the paediatric intensive care unit to check on Cody, that Jessica's cool professionalism and anxiety were flight responses? Was she trying to ignore the feelings and make them go away? If so, he could tell her it didn't work.

Using his swipe card, he let himself into PICU. Aside from the noise of the various monitoring machines and ventilators, the unit was quiet and dimly lit. He nodded to the charge nurse on duty and made his way to the bay that held Cody's bed. As he approached, he heard voices, one of which was Jessica's. He halted, surprised. What was she doing back here at this time of night? Curious, he listened before making his presence known.

'And when I think what could have happened,' Elsa Rowland commented, fear and guilt lacing her voice.

'You mustn't blame yourself, Elsa,' he heard Jessica respond softly, the gentle burr of her Scottish accent so attractive to him. 'A chronic subdural haematoma builds gradually. It can be weeks, even months, before the symptoms show. You did the right thing bringing Cody to A and E as soon as you realised something was wrong.'

'Thank you.' The woman's relief was tangible. 'I know Mr Corezzi explained it all to us but I didn't take anything in. And someone told me he's new. The thought of Cody's head being cut open is frightening.'

'Of course it is. But you can trust Mr Corezzi. He might be new to St Piran's but he's a very skilled and highly respected consultant neuro-surgeon and he's come to us from London with a tremendous reputation,' Jessica explained to the anxious woman, her glowing endorsement of him taking Gio by surprise.

'Cody looks so still and small. Are you sure everything is all right?' the tearful mother asked, and although Gio wanted to reassure her, he was keen to hear what Jessica would say.

'He's doing very well,' she replied, her tone conveying sympathy and authority. 'It's standard procedure for him to be in Intensive Care following the operation.'

Gio was impressed. He was also intrigued by the depth of Jessica's knowledge. She seemed too assured and informed for someone with no medical training.

'Ally's gone to get something to eat. The nurses want us to go home, but I can't bear to be away from Cody,' Elsa fretted.

'There's a cot in a room nearby for parents to use, and I'd advise you both to get what sleep you can there. But after tonight it would be best to get back into a normal routine. You and Ally need to keep strong so you are fit and ready to take Cody home,' Jessica urged, her common-sense approach pleasing him. 'I'll see you again tomorrow, but you can ring me if you need anything.'

There was a pause in the conversation and Gio waited a moment before making a sound and entering the bay. Elsa Rowland gave him a weary smile as he greeted her, but his attention immediately strayed to Jessica. She tensed, her gaze skittering to his and away again, a delicate flush of colour staining her cheeks.

As he checked Cody, who was sleeping peacefully, and looked over his chart, Gio was attuned to Jessica. What was she doing back at the hospital? Had she misled him when she'd said she was leaving for the day? He hoped to find answers as soon as Cody's father returned and, after a few pleasantries, Gio was able to escort Jessica out.

'I was surprised to see you,' he told her once

they had left the unit and were in no danger of being overheard. 'I thought you had left for the day.'

Once more a tinge of colour warmed her smooth cheeks. 'I had to rush home to meet the insurance company's assessor. I said I'd be back,' she added defensively, refusing to meet his gaze.

She *had* said that but he'd assumed she had meant the next day. Apparently unsure what to do with her hands now that she was no longer carrying the assorted paraphernalia he'd seen her with before, she pushed them into her skirt pockets.

'What about you? Why are you still here?'

Her questions cut across the electrically charged atmosphere that hummed between them.

'I was called in after a young woman was knocked down by a coach.' He gave her a brief summary of the events and the unsuccessful struggle in the operating theatre. 'Her injuries were too severe...there was nothing we could do.'

Jessica's expression softened, understanding

and sympathy visible in her olive-green eyes, and in her voice when she spoke. 'What a rotten end to your first day.'

'It could have finished on a better note,' Gio admitted with a rueful shrug, running the fingers of one hand through his hair.

Leaning back against the wall, Jessica met his gaze, and he witnessed her first real smile for him. *Dio*, but she was beautiful! The heavy weight settled back on his chest, making it difficult to breathe, and he felt each rapid thud of his heart.

'If it's not too late and you still want to talk about your patient...' Jessica's words trailed off and she bit her lip, looking hesitant and unsure.

'That would be good, thank you.' He'd take any opportunity to spend time with this elusive and most puzzling woman. 'Shall we go to the canteen? I've not eaten and the now congealed ready meal waiting in my microwave holds no appeal.'

Gio thought she was going to refuse and he found himself holding his breath as he waited for her answer. That it meant so much to him and he wanted so badly to be in her company should have worried him—*would* have worried him even one day ago. But in the short hours since he had met Jessica he felt changed somehow. Where this inexplicable but intense attraction was heading he had no idea, but he was keen to find out.

'All right.'

However reluctantly given, her agreement cheered him, and as he walked by her side down the deserted hospital corridor he felt as if he was setting out on one of the most important journeys of his life…with no map to help guide him and no clue as to the final destination.

CHAPTER THREE

'THAT wretched woman!'

Jess looked up in surprise as Brianna Flannigan, a nursing sister from the neonatal intensive care and special care baby units, banged a plate down on the canteen table and sat down, joining Megan and herself.

'What woman?' Jess and Megan asked in unison, concerned that the gentle, dedicated and softly spoken Brianna was so upset.

'Rita.'

Rita was the ward clerk in NICU/SCBU and renowned for nosing into other people's business, making her opinions, and often her disapproval, known. Few people took notice of her, but none wanted to fall under her spotlight. Both Brianna and Megan had suffered when Rita had picked on them in the past, and news she was hassling Brianna again brought out Jess's protective instincts.

'I'm sorry.' She sent her friend a sympathetic smile. 'What brought this on?'

Brianna idly pushed her salad around the plate. 'Now Diego and Izzy are no longer occupying Rita, she's refocused on me,' Brianna explained, frustration and displeasure in her lilting Irish voice.

'Tell her to mind her own business…that's what I do,' Megan riposted, stirring a sugar into her mug of tea. 'Not that it stops her. She's started making comments about me again, too.'

Jess knew Rita wasn't easily diverted once she set her mind on something. She suppressed a shiver. The idea of anyone probing into her past and her secrets was too awful to contemplate.

'She's always been nosy and judgemental. I thought she'd given up on me, but now she's asking where I came from and what I did before I joined St Piran's,' Brianna continued.

Jess recognised the dark shadows in her friend's brown eyes and couldn't help but wonder what had put them there.

'She'll never change,' Megan predicted. 'If she's not prying into someone's business, she's having a go about single mothers…or teenage ones. And don't get her started on her daughter.'

'What's wrong with her daughter?' Jess queried with a frown.

Megan dunked a biscuit in her tea. 'Nothing. That's the point. Marina's been happily married for twenty years and has several children—I've treated some of them for the usual childhood accidents and illnesses. They're a great family. Noisy and loving. Maybe that's what bugs Rita. She claims Marina married beneath her and shouldn't have had such a big family,' Megan finished, brushing crumbs from her lip.

'It's true she picks on Marina,' Brianna agreed. 'She finds fault with her grandchildren, too.'

The talk made Jess even more grateful that she had managed to avoid Rita's attention and speculation. Megan and Brianna were the closest she had to friends, yet they knew no more about her than she did about them, even after the years they had known each other. Which was probably why they got along so well. The mutual trust was there and they guarded each other's privacy, sharing an unspoken agreement not to ask personal questions, yet they could turn to one another should they need to, knowing their confidence would be respected.

'Rita's also asking questions about Gio Corezzi,' Brianna added, snapping Jess from her thoughts.

'Why would she start on him?' she asked, fighting a blush at the mention of Gio's name. 'She hasn't even met him, has she?'

Brianna nodded. 'She met him this morning. We all did. We have a baby with hydrocephalus—along with several other problems, the poor mite—and Richard Brooke called Gio up to the unit for advice,' the caring Irish woman explained, referring to the consultant who headed NICU.

'What sort of questions is Rita asking?' Jess queried, striving for casual indifference.

'She wants to know why someone who was such a wow in London would chose to "*bury himself*" in Cornwall,' Brianna told them, spearing some food with her fork. 'She saw Gio in the consultants' car park with James Alexander, chatting about cars—apparently they own the same model Aston Martin, but in different colours, so Rita's sure Gio's loaded.'

'For goodness' sake,' Megan responded, with the same disgust Jess was feeling.

'Rita asked Gio if his wife would be joining him here.' Brianna paused, and Jess steeled herself for what her friend would reveal next. 'Gio said, "Unfortunately not," and you could see the speculation in Rita's eyes until Gio added, after a deliberate pause, "She's *dead*." It was just awful. I felt terrible for him. He looked so sad. Even Rita was embarrassed, and that's saying something.'

As Brianna and Megan discussed Rita-avoidance tactics, Jess sat back and battled her emotions. Her heart squeezed with pain at the news of Gio's loss. Concerned for him, she also felt guilty for the unstoppable flicker of relief that he wasn't already taken. Not that *she* had any future with him. Or with anyone. But she couldn't help wondering what had happened…or question why he hadn't told her himself. Not that it was her business. She respected his privacy. And she hadn't told him *her* secrets.

Discovering how protective and possessive she felt of Gio was disconcerting. She knew the answer to some of Rita's questions, but she would never divulge them. Not even to Brianna and Megan. Not because they might gossip, they wouldn't, but for much more complicated reasons. She didn't want to admit to her friends, or to herself, how much she enjoyed and looked forward to Gio's company.

After Gio had returned to the hospital on the evening of his first day and had found her in PICU with the Rowlands, they had spent well over an hour in the canteen together. She'd had little time to wonder if he'd overheard any of her conversation with Cody's mother because she'd been pole-axed by the charge of electricity and blaze of sensual awareness that hit her every time she saw him. He'd looked gorgeous in jeans and a blue shirt, the shadow of stubble darkening his masculine jaw making him seem rakish and dangerous.

The canteen had been far less crowded than it was now, Jess acknowledged, shifting her chair in to allow a group of nurses to pass and access a nearby table. Gio had chosen a full meal, while she'd opted for a small bottle of mineral water and a packet of sandwiches...out of habit selecting things in disposable packaging. She hadn't budgeted for an extra snack, but as she'd not eaten anything but a banana and an apple since breakfast, she'd been hungry.

Having sunk everything she'd had into buying her cottage, she was counting every penny. The storm damage had been an unforeseen disaster but the insurance company was going to cover repairs for her roof despite the policy only being a month old. Having overstretched herself on the property, she was having to be frugal with everything else, not that she had hinted at the sorry state of her finances to Gio—or anyone else.

'Have you always worked here?' Gio had asked, turning their conversation that first night away from his patients and to work in general as he'd tucked into his dessert.

'No. I joined St Piran's when I was in the final year of my training,' she'd explained to him, amazed he'd found room for apple pie and cream after the large portion of lasagne that had preceded it. 'They asked me to stay on once I'd qualified.'

What she hadn't told him had been the extent of her relief that she'd not needed to move on again, something she had done several times since the life-changing bombshell had brought things crashing down around her. She'd carved out a niche for herself in St Piran, fulfilling a role that patients, relatives and staff all appreciated and which allowed her some welcome autonomy.

'You don't see patients in your office?' Gio had queried.

'Very rarely—although I have done so if circumstances required it,' she replied, thinking of Izzy, the young A and E doctor who, then six months pregnant, had wanted to return to work after taking leave following the traumatic time she had experienced.

It hadn't been easy, for Izzy or herself, but things had worked out well. Now Izzy had a beautiful baby girl and an amazing new man in her life in the shape of attractive Spaniard Diego, who had been a charge nurse in NICU/SCBU, and Jess wished them all the happiness in the world.

'My role is more immediate,' she had gone on to tell Gio. 'I give emergency help to those who need it, be that on the wards, in A and E, or elsewhere in the hospital.'

'Like the Rowlands.' Gio's smile had nearly stopped her heart.

'Y-yes.' Flustered, she'd tried to get a grip. 'There can be a wide variety of situations… parents making difficult decisions about treatment for their child, or a young man who has crashed his motorbike and, overnight, has gone from being fit and active to waking up in hospital to the news he'll never walk again. Or it could be an older person who's had a stroke and is unable to return to their home. Or a relative in A and E trying to come to terms with a sudden bereavement.'

Something dark and painful had flashed in Gio's intense blue eyes, alerting Jess to the possibility there had been some traumatic event in his past. She hadn't pried, and Gio had declined to refer to it, but she had wondered about his background.

'So you see people through those first stages?' he'd asked next, pushing his empty dish aside and reclaiming her attention.

'That's right. Sometimes people need a shoulder to cry on and a friend in their corner. Others need greater help and back-up. I can liaise with other departments and with agencies outside the hospital that can offer care, advice and support, like social services, or relatives who have expectations that the patient may not want,' she'd explained, finding him easy to talk to. 'My job is to support them and their rights, and to help them achieve the best solution to whatever problem they're facing. If they need ongoing counselling once they leave hospital, they are assigned to one of my colleagues through Outpatients, or to an outside support organisation.'

Gio had shaken his head. 'I hadn't realised the full extent of what you do for people. It's very impressive...*you're* very impressive. I can see why everyone here respects you so much.'

The admiration in his eyes and praise in his

sexy voice had warmed her right through and brought an uncharacteristic sting of tears to her eyes. 'It's hardly brain surgery,' she'd quipped to mask her embarrassment.

Gio's husky chuckle of appreciation had tightened the knot of awareness low in her tummy, and a sudden wave of longing had stolen her breath and made her realise how alone she had been these last four years. She enjoyed a friendship with Megan and Brianna, but it didn't extended beyond work and could never fill the cold and lonely void that had grown inside her since her life had turned upside down.

'Your first day's been hectic and hasn't ended in the best of ways, but how have you found St Piran's?' Jess had asked, anxious to move the conversation away from herself.

'I would rather not have returned to Theatre for that poor girl tonight,' he'd admitted, and she had seen the lines of tiredness around his eyes. 'But I've enjoyed today and it's good to be in near the beginning of a new unit for the hospital. It was one of the reasons I took the job. I was impressed with Gordon Ainsworth, the senior neurological consultant, the state-of-the-art equipment and the plans to increase the neurosurgical services here. Being able to help shape those services and build my own team appealed to me. Of course, many people cannot understand why I would leave London to come here.'

'It's none of their business, is it? If it's what you want, that's all that matters,' she'd told him, his surprised expression suggesting her matter-of-fact support had been in short supply.

'Thank you.' His slow, intimate smile had threatened to unravel her completely. 'St Piran's offered me new challenges and fresh opportunities, as well as the chance of more rapid career progression.'

It had made sense to her. 'Better to be a big fish in a small pond?'

Again the smile with its devastating effect on her. 'But it's much more than that...more than what I might gain for myself.' He'd leaned forward and folded his arms on the table, a pout of consideration shaping his sexy mouth. 'I commit a fair bit of time and money to a charitable trust that not only funds research, equipment for hospitals in various countries and support for patients and their families with brain tumours and other neurological conditions. We also bring children in desperate need of specialist treatment to the UK.'

She hadn't been surprised to learn of this side to him. She'd seen the kind of doctor he was. Instinct had told her how important the charity work was to him, and she'd suspected there was far more to it than he had told her…reasons why the trust was so close to his heart.

'That's fantastic. And it must be so rewarding.'

'It is. That St Piran's is interested and has given permission for me to continue to bring over a number of children each year, donating the hospital facilities free of charge, was a huge factor in my decision to come here.'

Jess had been fascinated as he'd talked more about the work he'd done with the trust. Her heart had swelled with pride as she'd thought about his selflessness and determination to use his skills to help others.

'He is *very* handsome, isn't he?'

Brianna's comment impinged on Jess's consciousness and she blinked, looking up and following her friend's gaze in time to see Gio carrying a tray across the canteen and sitting at a table with Ben Carter and James Alexander. Her pulse raced at the sight of him and she had to beat back a dart of jealousy at Brianna's evident appreciation of Gio's looks.

The man in question turned his head and met her gaze. For several moments it was as if there was no one else in the canteen—the myriad conversations going on all around her faded to a background hum and everything was a blur but Gio himself. A shiver ran down her spine and a very real sense of fear clutched at her. Less than a week and already this man had breached her defences and become all too important to her.

What was she going to do? If she allowed the friendship to develop, she knew things would end in heartbreak. Despite knowing that, and despite a desperate need to preserve all she had achieved these last four years, she wasn't sure she could give Gio up.

* * *

A sudden clatter and burst of laughter from across the room caught the attention of everyone in the canteen and snapped Gio's gaze away from Jessica. He glanced round in time to see three junior doctors trying to contain the mess from a can of fizzy drink as the liquid spewed from the top in a bubbly fountain, soaking everything and everyone within range.

'The Three Stooges,' Ben commented wryly.

James chuckled. 'Were we ever that young and foolish and confident?'

'Probably!' Ben allowed.

Gio tried not to dwell on the past. His memories were mixed, all the happy ones overshadowed by the bad ones and the blackest time of his life. Ben and James, fellow consultants with whom he had struck up an immediate rapport, began detailing the merits of the three rowdy young doctors, but Gio's attention was inexorably drawn back to Jessica. The now familiar awareness surged through him, tightening his gut and making it difficult to breathe.

Jessica was sitting with two other women. Megan Phillips, the paediatric registrar with

whom he worked frequently. And Brianna
Flannigan, a kind and dedicated nursing sister
in NICU/PICU, whom he'd met for the first time
that morning. On the surface, the three women
shared many similarities and yet they were dis-
tinctly different. And it was only Jessica who
made his pulse race and caused his heart, which
he had believed to be in permanent cold storage,
to flutter with long-forgotten excitement.

They had sat in this very canteen and talked for
a long time that first night, yet he'd discovered
precious little about her. He, on the other hand,
had revealed far more than he'd intended.

Her understanding and support about his move
to Cornwall had warmed him. Many people had
appreciated his need to leave Italy for New York
five years ago. Some had comprehended his decision to leave New York, and the team of the
neurosurgeon who had taught him so much, to
move to London. But very few had grasped why
he had chosen St Piran's over the other options
that had been open to him—options that would
have meant more money and working at bigger
hospitals.

Those things hadn't interested him, which had not surprised Jessica. St Piran's offered the opportunity of advancing to head of department within a decade, Gordon Ainsworth grooming him to take over when he retired, but it had been the administration's support of his charity work that had swayed his decision.

He'd told Jessica about the trust but *not* why it was so important to him. Not yet. That he was thinking of doing so showed how far she had burrowed under his skin. Even as warning bells rang in his head, suggesting he was getting too close too quickly, he couldn't stop himself craving her company and wanting to know more about her.

They'd seen each other often during the week, working together with a couple of new patients and a rapidly improving Cody Rowland. Their friendship grew tighter all the time but Jessica remained nervous. She'd relax for a time then something would cause her to raise her defensive wall again. Her working hours puzzled him, and the extent of her medical knowledge continued to intrigue him.

The little she had revealed about herself cen-
tred around her work at St Piran's. Listening to
her describe her role, and witnessing her way
with people—including the use of Charlie, the
teddy-bear hand puppet, to interact with frightened children—had left him full of admiration
for her devotion and skill.

'Much of my work involves supporting people
who face life changes and difficult decisions
caused by illness or accident. It's a huge shock
to the system,' she'd told him and, for a moment
her eyes had revealed such intense pain that it
had taken his breath away.

He'd wanted to comfort and hug her, but he'd
resisted the instinctive urge, aware of Jessica's
aversion to touching and being touched...one
of her mysteries he hoped to unravel. But the
incident had left him in little doubt that she'd
experienced some similar trauma. As had he, he
allowed, with his own dart of inner pain.

'Patients and relatives often try to be strong
for each other,' Jessica had continued with per-
ceptive insight, 'when often they need to admit
that they're scared and have a bloody good cry.'

She'd sent him a sweet, sad smile that had ripped at his already shredded heart. 'I'm merely a vehicle, a sounding board, someone outside their normal lives on whom they can offload all the emotion.'

What toll did that take on her? Gio wondered with concern. And who was there for her? They were questions to which he still had no answers.

Without conscious decision or prior arrangement, they'd met each evening in the canteen, lingering over something to eat, discussing work, finding all manner of common interests in books, music and politics, both of them steering clear of anything too personal.

He'd learned very quickly to tread carefully, watching for the triggers that caused her withdrawal. He liked her, enjoyed her company and was comfortable with her but also alive, aroused and challenged, feeling things he'd not experienced in the five long years since his world had come crashing down around him.

Taking things slowly was a necessity. For both of them. But every day he became more deeply

involved. So much so that having to say good-
night to her and return alone to his rented house
was becoming increasingly difficult.

'Oh, to be that young and free from responsibility.'

Edged with bitterness, the words were voiced
by Josh O'Hara and pulled Gio from his reverie.
The Irishman took the final empty chair and
set his plate down on the table. Gio regarded
the other man, wondering what had sparked his
reaction.

'Something wrong, Josh?' Ben asked, a frown
on his face.

'Bad day.' He pushed his food aside untouched.
'I've just had to DOA an eighteen-year-old...I
was going to say *man*, but he was scarcely more
than a boy with his whole life ahead of him.'

Gio sympathised, recalling how he'd felt
a few days ago when the young woman had
died in Theatre from multiple injuries. 'What
happened?'

'He was an apprentice mechanic at a local
garage, driving the work van and following another mechanic who was returning a customer's

car after service,' Josh explained, emotion in his accented voice as he told the story. 'Some bozo going home from a liquid lunch at the golf club and driving far too fast ploughed into the van. The boy wasn't wearing his seat belt, the van had no air-bags, and he went through the windscreen. He had horrible head and facial injuries—apparently he'd been a good-looking boy, not that I could tell—and a broken neck.'

Gio exchanged glances with Ben and James, both of whom were listening with equal solemnity and empathy. 'And the drunk driver?' Ben queried, voicing the question in all their minds.

'Yeah, well, there's the rub. There's no justice in this world.' Josh gave a humourless laugh. 'The boy's colleague, who witnessed the crash, is in shock. The drunk driver hasn't got a scratch on him. The police have arrested him and I hope they throw the book at him, but whatever sentence he gets won't be enough to make up for that young life, will it?'

'No,' Gio murmured with feeling.

As his three companions discussed the case,

Gio struggled to contain memories of another injustice and senseless loss of life, one he had been unable to prevent and which had plunged him into the darkest despair he had ever known. A darkness he had believed he would never escape. His gaze returned to Jessica, who, in just a few days, had brought flickerings of light and hope back into his life.

A shaft of sunshine from the window beside her made the vibrancy of her rich auburn hair gleam like pure flame. Brianna also had auburn hair but hers was a much lighter shade, lacking the coppery chestnut richness of Jessica's. Megan, whose hair was darker, was the tallest of the three, slender and fragile-looking. Brianna, an inch or two shorter, was lithe and athletic, while Jessica was shorter still and more rounded, her shapely feminine curves so appealing to him. She looked up and, as their gazes clashed once more, she sent him a tiny smile.

'From the Three Stooges to the Three Enigmas,' Ben remarked, his gaze following Gio's to Jessica's table, just as the rowdy young doctors left the canteen.

Fearing his new friend would detect his interest in Jessica, Gio dragged his gaze away and pretended not to know what Ben meant. 'Sorry?'

'Brianna, Jess and Megan,' Ben enlightened him. 'St Piran's Three Enigmas.'

'It's interesting that the three of them gravitated to each other,' James said, as he looked across at them.

Ben shrugged. 'I'm not surprised. They have so much in common. All three are intensely private and have somehow managed to elude the gossip-mongers. And all three have also ignored the attention showered on them by the majority of the single—and some not-so-single—men in the hospital. I don't think anyone knows anything more about them, or their lives outside work, than they did the day each of them began working here,' Ben finished.

'How long *has* Megan been here?' Josh asked, his apparent nonchalance only surface deep, Gio was sure.

'It must be, what…seven years? Maybe eight,' Ben pondered, and Gio noticed the set of Josh's jaw and the way he flinched, as if the time was somehow important.

Gio glanced over to Jessica's table again, his gaze resting a moment on Megan. He was just about to smile at her when he realised that she wasn't looking at him but at Josh. Pale faced and seemingly upset, Megan turned away.

Across from him Josh looked strained and affected by the silent exchange. There was a story there, Gio realised, but it was none of his business. He had enough to concern him settling into a new job, a new town, and dealing with the sudden and unexpected resurgence of his libido.

As the four of them prepared to return to their respective departments, their break over, Gio noticed activity at Jessica's table, too. She was standing up and reaching for her pager, a frown on her face as she read the message.

He wondered what had happened and who needed her now. Like a schoolboy with his first crush, he hoped he would meet up with Jessica later, craving the moments at the end of the day when he had her to himself, at least for a while.

She was becoming ever more important to him and he was both scared and excited to discover what was going to happen.

CHAPTER FOUR

As HER pager sounded, Jess rose to her feet, frowning as she read the call for her to attend A and E urgently.

'I have to go,' she explained as her friends said goodbye. 'I'll see you later.'

Jess squeezed her way between the tables, wishing she was as slender as Megan and Brianna. Before she left the canteen, she couldn't resist looking back at Gio. Her gaze clashed with his, delaying her, her footsteps slowing as if ruled by an inbuilt reluctance to leave him.

Gio waved, drawing Ben's attention as the men stood up from their table. Ben smiled at her, and she blushed, hoping he would think she was including all of them, and not that she had any special interest in Gio, as she sketched a wave in return and hurried out of the canteen.

As she made her way to A and E, her thoughts

remained with Gio. Beyond the dangerous attraction, she enjoyed his company, admired him, professionally and personally, and felt good with him. If she had any sense, she'd guard her heart and keep her distance, but she feared it was already too late. She'd begun to slide down the slippery slope by foolishly convincing herself it was OK to be friends with him…provided they both knew friendship was all it could be.

She knew Gio was curious and wanted to know more about her, but he'd been circumspect so far and she was grateful. Meeting in the canteen each evening challenged her resolve but his comments on how he hated returning to the empty house he was renting had touched a chord within her. She knew all about the loneliness found between the walls of somewhere that didn't feel like home. One more of the many things they had in common.

Arriving in A and E, Jess set thoughts of Gio aside. Ellen, a senior staff nurse in the department, greeted her and outlined the reason for the call.

'The girl came in very distressed, asking

after a young man killed in a road accident,' the middle-aged woman explained, shaking her head. 'She's terribly young, Jess, but she insists she's the girlfriend. Unfortunately we're rushed off our feet and as she's not physically injured or ill, we don't have time to spend with her, but we didn't want her to leave in such a state.'

'I understand. Has she been told anything?' Jess asked, her heart going out to the unknown girl.

Ellen sighed again. 'I'm afraid one of the in-experienced clerks told her the boyfriend, a lad named Colin Maddern, had died.'

'Oh, hell.'

'Exactly.' The nurse's displeasure matched her own. 'The girl wants Colin's things. He had no one but her. And there are photographs of her in his jacket, so she's genuine. I've checked with the police and they don't need anything, so I'll arrange to have the jacket and the possessions we salvaged brought to her.' Ellen nodded in the direction of the closed door to one of the quiet rooms used for relatives. 'She's in there. She wants to see him, but…'

'You don't think it's a good idea,' Jess finished for her.

'No, I don't. The poor boy wasn't wearing a seat belt and there was no air-bag fitted. He was hit at speed, went through the windscreen and was killed. A broken neck. And his face is a mess.'

Jess struggled to keep her emotions from showing. 'And the other driver?'

'Returning home drunk after lunch at the golf club. The police have arrested him. Needless to say he's not even bruised. Josh had to deal with both of them and he's furious. It's so unfair,' Ellen finished, mirroring Jess's own sentiments and explaining the grim expression on Josh's face when he'd arrived in the canteen.

'Do we know the girl's name?' Jess queried, jotting a few notes on her pad.

'No. Other than asking for Colin—and his things—she's not said anything. She broke down after she learnt of his death.'

'Thanks, Ellen.' She would not have relished the task of delivering the news, but Jess wished the girl had learned the truth in a more gentle and caring way. 'I'll see what I can do.'

The woman smiled. 'If anyone can help her, love, it's you.'

Jess hoped so. After Ellen had gone, she drew in a breath, hoping to find the right things to say in an impossible situation. Tapping on the door, she opened it and stepped inside. A junior nurse sat awkwardly near the sobbing girl, and jumped to her feet, clearly glad to leave.

Once they were alone, Jess pulled a chair closer and sat opposite the plump form huddled on the two-seater sofa. With her face buried in her hands, a curtain of straight, corn-coloured blonde hair swung forward, hiding her face from view. A cooling cup of tea remained untouched on the table beside her.

'Hello. I'm Jess Carmichael. I've come to see if there's anything I can help you with.' Jess waited for some kind of response or acknowledgement of her presence. 'I'm very sorry to hear about the accident.'

Slowly the girl looked up, her hands dropping away from her face and falling to her lap. Jess barely managed to smother a shocked gasp as she discovered how terribly young she was... no more than sixteen. Grey eyes were awash with tears, leaving no doubt at the depth of her devastation.

'They won't let me see him,' she murmured. 'Is it because I'm not officially family?'

Jess hesitated, unsure how to explain without causing further upset. 'It's a difficult decision. I'd urge you to think carefully, because once it's done, it can't be undone. They advised you against seeing Colin because of the nature of his injuries,' she continued, deciding it was important to tell the truth, even as the words caused the girl to flinch. 'Wouldn't you rather your last memory of him was a good one? What would he want for you?'

'Colin wouldn't want me to do it,' she admitted, a frown creasing her brow.

'There's no hurry to make a decision, so have a think about it.'

'OK.'

Jess hoped she would decide not to see him. 'Is

there someone I can call for you? Your parents, maybe?'

'No!' The denial was instant and accompanied by a vigorous shake of her head. 'I can't.' Taking a tissue from the box on the table, she blew her nose. 'No one knows about Colin and me.'

Jess let it go for now, not wanting to pressure the girl or distress her further, hoping instead to build rapport and a level of trust that would enable her to help if she could.

'Can you tell me your name?'

The girl fiddled nervously with the chain around her neck, suddenly clutching it before tucking it inside her blouse and doing up the top button, as if to hide it. Before Jess could consider the odd behaviour, the girl shifted nervously, her gaze darting around the room.

'Marcia Johns,' she finally offered, barely above a whisper.

'Thank you, Marcia.' Jess smiled, accepting the name, even though she was unsure at this point whether or not it was genuine. 'Would you like to talk about Colin?'

A firm nod greeted the suggestion, and

although tears shimmered in her eyes, a wobbly smile curved her mouth, revealing how pretty she could be. 'Yes, please. Is that OK?'

'Of course. I'd like to hear about him. When did you meet?'

'Over a year ago when I started my summer job,' she explained. 'Colin worked nearby. He was three years older than me, and never in a million years did I imagine him noticing *me*. Tall and handsome, with dark hair and blue eyes and a gorgeous smile, he was the one all the girls wanted. I'm shy and overweight and always fade into the background,' Marcia continued, revealing low self-esteem. She shook her head, as if in wonder, and gave a little laugh. 'When Colin began spending time with me, I couldn't believe it! There were all these thin, pretty girls chasing after him but he kept saying it was me he wanted, that he saw the real me inside. That I was kind and smart and funny, and he loved me the way I was.'

What a lovely young man, Jess thought, seeing how Marcia lit up talking about him. And what a terrible tragedy that his life had been cut so short. Sensing Marcia's need to talk, she encouraged her to continue.

'We were going to get married when I finished school and got a full-time job,' she said, toying with the friendship ring that encircled the middle finger of her right hand, no doubt a gift from him, Jess thought. 'His father died when he was twelve, and his mother when he was sixteen, so Colin had to look out for himself. He was much more responsible and steady than the boys I knew at school. There was never much money, but that didn't matter. We spent all our time together, walking on the beach, having picnics, watching DVDs or listening to music at his flat, talking for hours. Talking about everything. For the first time I felt as if someone really knew me and understood me.'

'Don't you feel that at home?' Jess probed, hoping to find out more about Marcia's background.

'Not really.' She gave a casual shrug, but it obviously mattered to her. 'We're a big family. My parents are busy working and caring for us all, and my brothers and sisters are all outgoing and active, and so much more attractive than I am. They all have the family colouring. I got the eyes but my hair is dead straight and mousy blonde. I'm interested in books and music, not sports. I don't understand them and they don't understand me. I know they love me,' she added, wiping away the twin tears that tracked down her rounded cheeks. 'They just don't *see* me. Everything is so hectic and noisy. I don't think they notice whether I'm there or not.'

'But Colin noticed.'

'Yes. Yes, he did.'

Jess understood how special and important the young man must have made Marcia feel, boosting her confidence and setting her free from the shadow of her vibrant family. Marcia might be very young, but she had a sensible head on her shoulders and for her, her relationship with Colin had been a close and genuine one.

Marcia pulled her shoulder bag on to her lap and rummaged inside for a moment before producing a couple of photos and handing them across.

'Thanks.'

Jess looked down at the first picture, seeing a very handsome young man dressed in jeans and a black leather jacket, wavy black hair brushing over the collar. The blue eyes were startling, full of intelligence, humour and kindness, his smile adding to the impression of warmth and friendliness. The second picture, of Marcia and Colin together, banished any lingering doubt about the full extent of this young girl's relationship with Colin. No one seeing the two young people together could question their feelings. Their happiness and love shone out, and the expression of devotion on Colin's face as he looked at a laughing Marcia brought a lump to Jess's throat.

'They're lovely. Thank you for showing me,' she murmured, handing the pictures back.

Marcia looked at them for several moments before tucking them carefully back in her bag. She sobbed, pressing a hand to her mouth, despair in her eyes.

'What am I going to do?' Rocking back and forth, tears flowed in earnest once more. 'Colin was my whole life. I love him so much. And I need him. He can't be gone. He *can't*. It isn't fair. Oh, God… Why? *Why* has this happened? What's the point in anything if Colin isn't with me?'

As she tried to comfort the girl, Jess wished she had answers to explain the cruel and senseless loss of a life. Fresh anger built within her at the driver who had thoughtlessly climbed behind the wheel of his car, his selfish actions shattering two young lives. He should be made to see Colin's lifeless, damaged body, and witness the terrible grief Marcia was suffering. What words could she possibly offer the girl that didn't sound trite?

A knock at the door announced the arrival of Ellen and provided a welcome distraction. 'May I come in?'

As Marcia nodded and mopped her tears, Jess met the kindly nurse's gaze, seeing the sympathy and sorrow in her eyes.

'I have Colin's things for you, love,' Ellen said, setting a black leather jacket on the seat beside Marcia, the same jacket Colin had worn in the photos.

Marcia drew the jacket into her arms, closing her eyes and burying her face in the wear-worn leather. 'I saved up for ages to buy this for his birthday. It smells of him,' she whispered, clutching the familiar garment more tightly to her and rubbing one cheek against it.

A lump in her throat, Jess exchanged a glance with Ellen. Maybe having Colin's jacket would bring Marcia some comfort and familiarity in the difficult times ahead.

'Here are the photographs and the other things Colin had with him,' Ellen said, holding over a large padded envelope.

Refusing to let go of the jacket, Marcia took the envelope with her free hand. 'Thank you, it means a lot. And thanks for being so kind to me.'

'You're welcome, my love.' Suppressed emotion made Ellen's voice huskier than normal. 'I'm so sorry.'

After Ellen had left them alone once more, Jess allowed Marcia some quiet time. While she waited, she took a page from her notebook and jotted down some information for the girl to take away with her.

'I don't like to think of you going home alone, Marcia. You've had a horrible shock. Are you sure I can't call your parents? Or I could arrange for someone here to take you home,' Jess suggested, willing to drive her there herself, but Marcia was withdrawing and shaking her head.

'No. No, I don't want that.' She took another tissue and mopped her eyes. 'Thank you. I'll be all right.'

Jess didn't believe it for a moment, but she couldn't force her and she didn't want to break the tentative trust between them. All she could do was encourage Marcia to keep in touch.

'You can contact me here at any time, Marcia,' she told her, adding another telephone number to the list. 'I've also given the details for the Samaritans. If you need to talk to anyone in confidence, day or night, you can call them. I volunteer once a week, usually on Friday evenings, but you can talk freely to anyone.'

'OK.'

Jess was relieved as Marcia took the sheet of paper, looked it over, and then tucked it into her bag, suggesting she might actually use it and not toss it into the first litter bin she came across.

'I'd really like to know how you are. And if there's anything I can do...' She let the words trail off, not wanting to nag.

The sound of her pager intruded. Smothering her frustration, Jess checked the display before glancing around the room and discovering there was no telephone.

'I've taken up too much of your time,' Marcia murmured, beginning to gather her things together.

'No, no, it's fine, honestly.' Jess smiled and told a white lie. 'I'm not in a hurry. I just have to reply to this. If you don't mind waiting, I'll just pop into the next door room to use the phone. I'll be back in a jiffy.'

Jess found a phone and made the call. She doubted she'd been gone more than a minute, but by the time she returned, Marcia had gone.

'Damn it!'

Upset, she rushed down the corridor and back

into the busy casualty department, asking a couple of nurses and the clerks at the desk if they had seen Marcia come though, but no one had noticed her. Not even the security guard by the main doors. It brought back Marcia's own words…she faded into the background and no one saw her.

Cursing the appalling timing of the interruption, Jess went outside, hoping to catch a glimpse of Marcia, but it was hopeless. The sense of disappointment was huge. She couldn't bear to think of Marcia alone with her grief, unable and unwilling to seek the comfort of a family who loved her but seldom had time for her.

An image of Marcia and Colin before the tragedy, so happy and in love, fixed itself in her mind. Why did awful things happen? She could make no sense of the cruelty that had befallen two lovely young people. She swallowed, blinking back tears.

'Jessica, are you all right?'

Gio's voice behind her had her spinning round in surprise. 'What are you doing here?'

'I was in A and E and saw you run outside.'

The expression in his blue eyes, so warm and intimate, robbed her of breath and held her captive as he raised a hand and with exquisite gentleness removed a salty bead of moisture suspended from her lashes, his fingers brushing her cheek. His voice turned even huskier. 'I was worried about you.'

Everything in her screamed at her to lean into his touch, craving what she had denied herself for so long, but reality intruded, the instinct for self-preservation ingrained. She jerked back, feeling the colour staining her cheeks as Gio regarded her in silence, speculation, concern and a frightening resolve in his eyes.

'Tell me what's wrong,' he invited as they headed back to the hospital.

Sighing, Jess gave him a brief summary of what had happened, unable to prevent her emotion from showing. 'It was just awful.'

'I'm sorry.' He shook his head, murmuring what sounded like a curse in Italian. 'Josh was talking about the accident in the canteen.'

Back in the room where she had spoken with Marcia, Gio remained with her, increasing her sense of awareness. 'I feel as if I failed her,' she admitted.

'Of course you didn't,' he chided gently.

'I don't know.' With another sigh, she gathered up her things. 'I'm even more sure now that Marcia Johns is not her real name.'

'Definitely not.'

The edge of amusement in Gio's voice had her head snapping up. There was nothing remotely funny about the situation. But before she could remonstrate with him, he shook his head and pointed to something behind her. She turned round, noticing for the first time the information posters on one wall of the room.

The 'infomercials' were sponsored by well-known drug companies and 'Marcia' had been clever enough, despite her distress, to cobble together a false name on the spur of the moment, using parts of two words from the company name emblazoned in large letters on one of the posters. Jess cursed herself for having been so thoroughly duped. She was also disappointed that the girl had felt the need to deceive her.

'She had her reasons, and I'm sure they were personal to her and nothing to do with you.'

Jess knew Gio's words were offered by way of consolation, but they did little to ease her upset and concern. 'Marcia' would remain in her thoughts and she would worry about her unless and until she had any further news of her. She could only hope that at some point the girl would use one of the contact numbers she had given her and get in touch.

'I know how much you care,' Gio said now, scarily attuned to her thoughts. 'You would not be so good at your job if you didn't, but you cannot carry the burden of everyone's problems on your shoulders, Jessica.' He stood in front of her, tipping her chin up with one finger until her gaze met his. 'Who is there for you?'

She felt branded by the contact and once more she stepped back to break it, resisting the urge to press her free hand to the spot that still tingled from the soft touch of his fingertip. This was ridiculous! She needed to give herself a stern talking to. Squaring her shoulders, she headed for the door.

'I'm fine,' she told him, injecting as much firmness into her voice as possible.

'You are here at all hours, taking on the burden of everyone else's problems,' he continued, refusing to let it go. 'Who listens to yours?'

Frightened that his perceptiveness and caring were chipping away at the defences that had protected her these last four years, she laughed off his question and repeated the words she used as a mantra to convince others...and herself. 'I'm fine!'

He took her by surprise—again—politely opening the door for her and following her out. So grateful was she that he had let the subject drop, she was not adequately on her guard.

'Where are you going now?' he asked.

'Hmm...' Jess frowned, trying to remember what had been on her agenda before the call had come in for her to attend A and E.

'If you have a few minutes to stop off at my office, I have some things to discuss with you.'

Although she would sooner have parted company there and then so she had time to re-erect her barriers against him, she was relieved he had focused back on work matters. Cursing her weakness and the voice in her head that tormented her about her vulnerability to this man, Jess found herself assenting to his request.

'All right.'

'Thank you.'

His smile of satisfaction made her uneasy. What had she agreed to? And why did she feel he'd set her up and she'd fallen for it—as she feared she had for him—hook, line and sinker?

CHAPTER FIVE

'COME this way.'

Jess found herself ushered into Gio's office, his hand at the small of her back sending a charge of electricity zinging through her. He had a disturbing habit of touching her. As he closed the door, Jess took the opportunity to put some much-needed distance between them. The room was by no means small but, confined in it with Gio, it seemed claustrophobic and she felt an urgent need for the comfort of her own personal space.

'What I am about to reveal to you is strictly confidential, Ms Carmichael. You do realise that?' he asked, his expression sombre...but for a tell-tale glimmer of mischief in his tanzanite-blue eyes.

Jess had no idea whether he was serious, or whether he was toying with her. Why did just

being in the same room with him make her feel
so off kilter and peculiar? She didn't like it. What
she most wanted was to escape.

'Jessica?'

She jumped, continually unnerved at the way
he spoke her name, his husky, accented voice far
too intimate and intoxicating. But it was the light
touch of one finger on her forearm that brought
her inbuilt flight response into action again as
she stepped back, distracted by the way all her
nerve-endings were fired into life. Startled, she
met the intense blueness of his gaze, seeing the
curiosity, knowledge and masculine appreciation
that lurked in his eyes. She didn't want anyone
interested in her or asking questions about her,
least of all this man who posed a unique and
definite danger.

'What's confidential?' she queried, intrigued
and yet nervous.

'Apart from my secretary, no one knows about
this. I'm trusting you, Jessica.'

'Yes, of course.' She agreed without hesitation. It was asked of her, in one way or another,
every working day, either by a patient, relative or

colleague. And very little surprised her. 'What is it?'

Gio moved to his desk and beckoned her closer. She edged forward, watching as he opened the bottom drawer of his desk, pulling it back with frustrating slowness, building her suspense as centimetre by centimetre the contents came into view.

She'd been wrong to believe he couldn't surprise her. Her eyes widened in astonishment as she found herself staring at a drawer full to the brim with...

'Chocolate!'

Gio couldn't help but laugh aloud at Jessica's stunned reaction. 'What is your poison? Plain or milk? With or without nuts?' he asked, taking a selection of bars from the drawer.

'I don't eat much chocolate.'

'But you like it,' he prompted, hearing the waver in her voice. 'You must do...given the delicious scent of your hair and your skin.'

His words brought a bloom of colour to her porcelain cheeks. But it was the longing in her eyes that betrayed her sweet tooth. And then her pink tongue-tip peeped out to moisten the sensual curve of her lips, causing his body to react in such an immediate and blatant way that he drew back in shock.

'Treat yourself,' he encouraged, thankful that she appeared unaware of his response to her and, as he waited for her to make her selection, struggled to get his mind and body back under control.

'OK.' She took a small bar of milk chocolate with a hazelnut praline centre. 'Thank you.'

'Good choice,' he murmured as she moved away.

Taking a bar of dark chocolate with almond for himself, he put the rest away and closed the drawer. Sitting down, he opened his chocolate, his gaze remaining on Jessica as she inspected the expensive high-class packaging, noting the moment realisation dawned.

'*Cioccolato Corezzi?*' She looked up, stunning green eyes wide with interest. '*You* make this chocolate?'

'My family do. My paternal grandfather began

the company over fifty years ago, and Papá and Mamma have grown it from a small specialist business with one shop in Turin into what it is today—one of Italy's most famous hand-made chocolate houses.'

'You're understandably proud of them.' She smiled, snapping off a square and popping it into her mouth, nearly killing him as those mesmerising eyes closed and a blissful look transformed her face as she savoured the flavours he knew would be bursting on her tongue. 'Oh, this is *amazing*!'

'Thank you.' Her opinion was important to him and her enthusiasm made him feel warm inside.

Snapping off another square, she laughed. 'No, thank *you*!' she insisted, before popping the chocolate into her mouth to savour the taste as before.

It was the first time he'd heard her laugh. It was a warm, throaty, infectious sound and he wanted to hear it often. Frowning, he acknowledged just how involved he was becoming.

'Did you never want to follow in your parents'

footsteps?' she queried after a moment, perching on the edge of his desk, stretching her skirt across the pleasing curve of womanly thighs.

'No,' he answered, his voice rough. Clearing his throat, he sat forward. 'It was never an option, and my parents knew it wouldn't have suited me. Besides, I would have eaten all the profits!'

Taking a bite of his chocolate, he enjoyed another of her throaty chuckles.

'You must have lorry loads of it delivered, judging by your drawer!'

Having her relax enough to tease him was an unexpected pleasure, as was listening to the softness of her accent. He wondered how she had come to be in Cornwall, so far from home, but he refrained from asking...for now.

'Now you know my secret,' he said, keeping his tone light and teasing. 'It's only fair you tell me one of yours, no?'

The change in her was immediate and, while he regretted her withdrawal and the loss of their rapport, he was intrigued by her reaction and eager to find out its cause. Her whole body tensed, as if she was closing in on herself. Sliding off the desk, she turned away, but not before he had seen the hurt and loneliness she worked hard to hide. Stepping across to the window, her shoulders lifted as she breathed in a slow, deep breath. Finally, she turned round, popping the last piece of chocolate in her mouth and scrunching up the wrapper.

'I'm not very interesting, and I don't really have any secrets,' she told him with a manufactured smile, not meeting his gaze.

Oh, but she most certainly did. He knew it. And he was determined to uncover them and understand what she was anxious to hide. Behind the façade she presented to the world, the real Jessica was far from fine.

'I ought to be going,' she announced, picking up the collection of items she had with her all the time in the hospital.

'What *do* you carry around in there?' he asked with a mix of interest and amusement.

Her voice sounded strained now, all traces of the fun Jessica reined in and back behind her protective wall. 'I have my notebook and diary,' she began, looking down at the pile in her arms.

Gio listened as she told him about the information sheets, details of various diseases and injuries and their treatments, names and contacts for self-help groups and a welter of other things people might need. Her mobile phone, like her pager, was either attached to her waistband or in her pocket, depending on the clothes she was wearing. He suspected Jessica used the things she carried as a barrier, a shield between herself and others. He wanted to know why. The list of questions he had about her continued to grow.

Disappointment speared inside him as Jessica moved towards the door. 'Thanks for the chocolate.'

'Any time. I'll tell my secretary you have free access to my secret drawer.' He smiled, drinking in his fill of her while he could. 'See you later. And try not to worry about your girl.'

'I'll try. Bye.'

The door closed softly behind her. At once the room felt different...and he felt lonely without the vibrancy of her presence. *Dio.* A week ago, if anyone had told him he'd be attracted to another woman, he would have believed it impossible. But Jessica had shaken him to his foundations— and out of the darkness that had enveloped his life for the last five years.

'Megan, are you all right?'

'Yes.' It was a lie, but she managed a smile for Jess. 'I'm sorry, I was miles away.'

Her friend sent her an understanding smile. 'Josh?'

'Yes,' Megan repeated, a deep sigh escaping.

It had been a huge shock to discover that Josh had joined the St Piran's trauma team back in the spring. Megan had assumed he was still in London. Wished he *was* still in London. Working with him when she was on call to A and E from Paediatrics was difficult and she had found it harder still since little Toby's funeral.

'He wants to talk,' Megan confided, her recent confrontation with Josh in the canteen still fresh in her mind. Why did he want to rake over the past? Did he think she didn't live with it every day of her life?

'Would talking to Josh be such a bad thing?'

Megan's stomach churned in response to Jess's softly voiced question. Her friend knew there was past history with Josh, but Megan hadn't divulged any details. She had never told anyone what had happened. She felt too guilty, too confused, too stupid, too hurt.

'What's the point?' Bitterness laced her voice but she was unable to soften it. 'It's over. Done. What good would be served stirring it up eight years on?'

'Perhaps *you* need to talk as much as Josh thinks *he* does,' Jess suggested, confusing her more.

Megan frowned. 'What do you mean?'

'It's clearly still causing you heartache. Things are unresolved in your own mind.' Jess paused a moment, her dark green gaze direct. 'Forget Josh and his reasons for wanting to talk. Think about yourself. Do *you* have questions that need answering before you can put things behind you once and for all?'

Too many to count, Megan allowed silently, one hand unconsciously moving to press against the flatness of her belly, a wave of pain rolling through her at all that was lost—all that Josh had taken from her. The thought of facing him after eight years was too scary to contemplate.

'Maybe, but—' Megan broke off, uncertain and indecisive.

'But?' Jess probed gently.

'Seeing him again hurts so much and has brought back so many difficult memories.' She bit her lip, ashamed that she had been so foolish over Josh—and that part of her remained drawn to him, despite everything that had happened. 'I'm so angry with him, Jess. And with myself. Yes, there are things I want to know, but I'm not sure I can cope with what he has to say.'

'Only you can decide if finding out what you need to know will help you find peace with the past.'

Megan nodded. Her friend's words made sense. She just wasn't sure what to do. The fact that Josh now had a picture-perfect wife, aside from causing her added pain and distress, complicated things even more. Although the body language she had witnessed between him and his beautiful wife, Rebecca, suggested that things might not be right in Josh's marriage, he *was* married, so having contact with him beyond the professional was inappropriate.

'It scares me, Jess.'

Her words whispered from her as she faced the awful truth—underneath the pain, anger and betrayal, a spark of the elemental chemistry still burned. She was as vulnerable to him as she had always been.

'Emotions are complicated and the dividing line between love and hate can be wafer thin.' Jess's pager sounded and she glanced at it, a faint blush colouring her cheeks. 'Sorry, Megan, I have to go.'

'Problems?'

Jess shook her head. 'It's time for the neurosurgery case meeting. Gordon Ainsworth and, um, Gio, asked me to attend,' she explained, gathering up her things. Pausing, she smiled. 'Think things over. If you need to talk, you know it will remain confidential between us.'

'Thanks, Jess.'

'Take care, Megan. And good luck.'

Megan watched the other woman walk away,

her vibrant auburn hair restrained in a plait. Recalling her friend's blush, and thinking about the electric atmosphere she had noticed whenever Jess and Gio were together, she wondered if something was brewing there. It would be wonderful to see Jess happy. She was so private, and always seemed so alone. Megan shook her head, realising how alike they were. She respected Jess, and trusted her, and she knew how lucky she was to have her to talk to.

Unfortunately, her friend couldn't tell her what to do. No one could. Decisions about Josh, and whether to face the past, were hers alone.

Gio stepped into the warmth of the August evening. Dusk was falling, and he glanced up at the darkening sky, expelling a sigh. He'd been called in earlier that Saturday evening after Josh O'Hara's concern had grown about a man who had collapsed while on an outing to the beach with his wife. Further tests, including CT and MRI scans, had revealed that the man had a tumour growing in his brain, affecting his optic nerve and sensory centre. Surgery was scheduled for Monday.

The man and his wife would benefit from Jessica's input. He'd speak with her on Monday. Which was nearly thirty-six hours away and too long to wait, especially as he hadn't seen her since the previous afternoon, when she had attended what would become a regular Friday meeting for the neurological unit. Her presence had been beneficial to the team—but distracting for him on a personal level. He shook his head. Until a few days ago he hadn't *had* a personal level.

Confused that his life had turned upside down, he walked towards the almost deserted consultants' car park. The previous night had been the first when they'd not met up for an end-of-the-day chat. Jessica had been unable to come because she volunteered for the Samaritans and spent several hours there each Friday evening. He wasn't surprised. Once more she was devoting her time to other people's problems. Was it a way of avoiding her own?

In the car, he leaned back and rested his head,

reflecting on how long and lonely the weekend was becoming without Jessica. He swore softly to himself. What a sorry state he was in. Part of him rebelled. He didn't want any new woman in his life. Or so he had thought until Jessica. Now he couldn't stop thinking about her or wanting to be with her. He wanted to learn her secrets and encourage the real Jessica out from behind her defensive wall. Was he the only one to notice the loneliness and hurt that lurked in the depths of her beautiful green eyes?

Starting the engine, he reversed out of his parking space, his gaze straying to the psychology building.

'What the hell?'

He braked, letting the powerful engine idle as he observed the light that shone from Jessica's office window. The rest of the building was in darkness. Had she forgotten to switch off the light the day before? He saw a flicker of movement inside and cursed. Jessica was here? *Now?* Returning his car to its parking space, he switched off the engine, climbed out and locked the door.

As he walked towards the building he reflected on Jessica's odd behaviour and her reluctance to let him see inside her office. He'd brushed it off as a quirk, but her furtiveness made him certain that something more was going on and he couldn't let this go.

Frowning, he remembered when he'd visited her office. She'd rushed home to meet her insurance company's assessor and he'd forgotten to ask why. Was something seriously wrong?

The outer door of the psychology building was locked, but his swipe card and ID code gained him access. Relocking the door, he made his way through the darkened foyer and down the corridor to Jessica's room. It was uncharacteristic for him to be impolite but, not wanting to give her time to shut the door in his face, he checked to see if it was unlocked. It was. He gave a sharp rap and swung the door open, astonished at the scene that greeted him.

Jessica, bare-footed and dressed in a pair of cotton shorts and a sleeveless tank top, which emphasised her voluptuous curves and set his pulse racing, was sitting cross-legged on a blow-up mattress on the floor. A pillow and a few items of bed linen were folded at one end. For the first time, he saw her hair in all its heart-stopping glory as it fell around her shoulders, the curtain of copper-red and burnished chestnut curls enveloping her in a halo of fire.

But she was not alone. Her companions held him transfixed and momentarily speechless. Two small, playful kittens frolicked around her, Tabby balls of fluff on stubby legs and paws that looked too big for them. His gaze returned to Jessica. The smile had frozen on her face and panic was setting in.

Determined to discover what was going on, but not wanting to alarm her, he closed the door and crossed to her before she had time to get up. He dropped to his knees, sitting back on his heels, smiling as the kittens investigated him, sharp claws digging into his thighs as they used him as a climbing frame.

Gently, he slid a palm under each warm, rounded little body, lifting them close for a better view, seeing the similarities and differences in what were clearly siblings' faces. He loved animals, and would have surrounded himself with them, but Sofia had been allergic to several kinds of animals, making pets impossible. Thinking of his beloved wife, taken from him so devastatingly five years before, brought the familiar pain and he closed his eyes, rubbing his face against the two fluffy animals, feeling the dual purrs vibrating against his hands.

Gio opened his eyes and focused on Jessica, who sat little more than a foot away, shocked to silence, a whole mixture of emotions chasing themselves across her expressive green eyes. Turning the kittens so they were facing her, he held them against his chest, enjoying their softness and the feel of their heartbeats.

'What are their names?'

His question apparently threw her because she stared at him for several moments as if expecting him to launch into an interrogation. She bit her lip, diverting his attention to the tempting swell of her mouth. As she sucked in a breath, his gaze rose to clash with hers once more.

'Th-that's Dickens,' she finally informed him, her voice unsteady and her hand shaking as she pointed to the kitten in his left hand, which had a dark face, pink nose and round green eyes, not unlike her own in colour.

'And this one?' he asked of the kitten in his right hand, which had slanting, almond-shaped eyes in a darker shade than its sibling's.

'Kipling.'

She looked lost and alone so he handed Dickens to her, and she clutched him close as if needing the comfort.

'They are favourite authors of yours?'

Jessica nodded, her curls swaying like dancing flames. 'Partly. But also for their characters. They're very mischievous and inquisitive. With him,' she continued, pointing to the kitten cradled in his hands, 'I kept thinking he's just so naughty, just so cute, just so everything, and so I thought of Kipling and his *Just So* stories.' She was still tense, but a smile tugged her mouth as she looked at the kitten she held. 'This one was into everything and I was always asking what the dickens he was up to. The names stuck.'

'How long have you had them?'

'About six weeks. Their mother was an

unknown feral stray who had a litter in the barn on a farm near my cottage,' she told him, relaxing a little. 'Flora, who lives there, and who is a nurse at the doctors' surgery in Penhally, isn't sure what happened to the mother, but the kittens were abandoned and Flora took care of them. She couldn't keep them all and was looking for homes for the others. I took these two.'

'What happens to them during the day?' he asked, intrigued how she had organised things.

'They stay with Sid Evans—he's the hospital handyman.' Gio nodded, confirming he knew of the man. 'He lost his wife recently and I've spent some time chatting to him,' Jessica continued, although he was unsurprised to learn of her kindness. 'He was very down and told me he wasn't allowed pets at his flat. So I asked the hospital management if he could have the kittens in his work room during the day and they said yes.' A warm smile curved her mouth. 'Sid loves having them.'

'I'm sure he does.' He admired her even more for her thoughtfulness. He also suspected that Jessica had set things up so that Sid felt valued, believing he was doing her a good turn. He was sure the hospital management didn't know where the kittens spent the night. 'How long have you been camping here?'

His question, getting to the core of the issue, had her tensing up again and she ducked her head, her hair falling forward, hiding her face.

'Talk to me,' he encouraged softly. With one finger beneath her chin, he urged her to look up again. 'What's going on, Jessica?'

Very conscious of Gio's touch, Jess trembled. The pad of one finger, that was all, and yet her whole body felt alive, charged and vitally aware of him. It was so long since she'd been touched… at least before this week when Gio had done so several times, stirring up desires she'd managed to banish for the last four years. But she had to quash the yearnings Gio had reawakened because he—like everyone else—was out of bounds. Steeling herself, she drew back enough to break the physical connection, concerned how much she missed the contact.

In shock from Gio's sudden arrival, fear built

now that one of her secrets, albeit the least monumental and important of them, had been discovered. She didn't want to tell him anything but how could she bluff her way out? Even if she could excuse the kittens, the damning evidence of the makeshift bed was impossible to explain away.

'Jessica?'

'I, um, recently moved into my cottage,' she began shakily, unsure how much to tell him. 'The storm ten days ago destroyed the roof, causing water damage and the electricity being shut off. I tried to say there anyway...'

'*Dio!* With no power and no roof?' he exclaimed, muttering something uncomplimentary in Italian.

Jess lowered her gaze. 'It was only one night. I was concerned for the kittens,' she explained, failing to add that not only had it been miserable with no electricity or hot water but that she'd been spooked in the isolated cottage with no security.

'So you've been staying here since then?'

'Yes,' she admitted with reluctance.

She couldn't help but be mesmerised by the way Gio continued to stroke Dickens, his fingers sinking into the soft fur. The kitten was enjoying it if his purrs were anything to go by. It made her think dangerous and never-to-be-allowed things...like how it would feel to have Gio's fingers caress *her* body from top to toe. She had no doubt she'd be purring, too.

Looking down lest he read anything in her eyes, Jess struggled to push her wayward thoughts away because no matter how much she may crave his touch, it wasn't going to happen.

'Why here, though?' Gio's voice reclaimed her attention. 'Why not stay at a hotel...or with friends?'

She fudged an answer, mumbling about the need to keep the kittens with her and everywhere being fully booked at the height of the season, because no way was she going to tell him the truth about the sorry state of her finances or that she didn't *have* any friends. Not the kind she could stay with, anyway. To explain either would involve the impossible—revealing what she could never reveal...*why.*

Why she had crashed and burned so badly...

Why her life had changed so drastically and irrevocably four years ago...

And why she was now counting the cost in so many ways, not just financially but professionally—hence her change of career and re-training in her mid-twenties to become a counsellor—and socially—keeping people at a distance and denying herself the closeness, emotional or physical, she had once enjoyed as a normal part of life. Nothing about her life these last four years had been normal. But she'd succeeded, she was coping...or had been until Gio had arrived, bringing home all she had lost and making her yearn for things she could never have again.

'It's only for a short while.' She crossed her fingers, hoping that was true. 'The insurance company have agreed to the repairs and the builders are starting work next week. As soon as possible, I'll move back in.'

'You can't stay here and live like this until then, Jessica,' he protested, clearly upset about the situation.

'It's not so bad,' she countered, trying for a carefree smile. 'I don't have any choice.'

'Of course you do.'

His words and the determined tone of his voice made her nervous. 'What do you mean?'

'As of now, you're moving in with me.'

CHAPTER SIX

UNOBSERVED, Gio leaned against the doorjamb and watched as Jessica carried out some graceful Tai Chi movements. She was dressed in a loose T-shirt, shorts that left shapely legs bare from mid-thigh down, and a pair of trainers, her vibrant curls restrained in a ponytail. He never tired of looking at her. Taking a sip of his coffee, he waited for her to finish her routine.

It was the August bank holiday weekend and they both had two days off. Jessica had been in his house for two weeks. She'd protested, but there had never been any question in his mind about where she should stay. He couldn't let her camp in her office. She'd wanted to pay rent, he'd said no, but they'd compromised and she made a contribution towards food and supplies.

She'd also set rules. No touching. And nothing more than a platonic friendship. He'd agreed.

Sort of. Temporarily. If setting them and keeping things on a friendly footing was what Jessica needed to begin with, he would play along. For now. That she'd felt the need to make rules at all proved she felt the same electric awareness he did.

He was using the time to gain Jessica's trust and continuing to get her used to his touch. He stopped the moment she withdrew or showed signs of disquiet. As the days went by, it was taking her longer to step away. He had yet to discover why she struggled so hard to deny the attraction.

Having coaxed her and the kittens home that Saturday night, the next day they had driven to her cottage. He'd grown up bilingual thanks to his parents and his American-born maternal grandmother, but, however fluent he was in English, he swore best in Italian and he'd unconsciously reverted to his native language as he surveyed the state of Jessica's home. It had been far worse than he'd imagined.

Built of stone and sitting in an isolated spot surrounded by untended land, the large cottage was single storey. The thatched roof and rotten rafters had collapsed inwards, wrecking several rooms beneath, letting in the rain and rendering the place uninhabitable. He'd seen the promise, had visualised the picture-book traditional cottage as it would be when it was finished, but that Jessica had tried to stay in what was little more than a ruin had astounded him.

Turning round, he'd seen the pained expression on Jessica's face, and realised the effect his rant was having on her. Reverting to English, he'd gentled his tone and closed the gap between them. His nature was to touch, to hug, to comfort, and it had been difficult to stop himself from drawing her into his arms.

Slowly he'd raised one hand and cupped her cheek, marvelling at the peachy softness of her skin. 'I'm sorry. I was not shouting at you, just at the state of the place and knowing someone would sell it to you in such a perilous condition.'

Some of the tension had drained from her, and for a second she'd leaned into his touch. He'd brushed the pad of his thumb across the little hollow between her chin and her mouth, watching as her lips had parted instinctively and her eyelids lowered in response. She hadn't actually purred like one of the kittens, but her reaction had been unmistakeable. He'd so wanted to kiss her, but the moment had ended as she'd withdrawn into herself, turning her head away to break the contact.

'If the cottage had been in better condition I couldn't have afforded it,' she'd told him. 'I knew the roof was dodgy...' She'd given a wry laugh as she'd looked at the blue sky visible between what remained of the rotten rafters. 'I didn't expect it to cave in with the first storm.'

He'd never had to worry about money, and he knew how lucky he was, never taking things for granted. The business had made his family wealthy and money cushioned many blows. Except grief. Nothing eased the pain of that, but at least he'd been in a position to fund the trust in Sofia's name and help other people. He hated to think of Jessica struggling to make ends meet, and wondered why she had apparently sunk every penny she'd had into such a run-down, if potentially lovely, cottage, with no money left over to furnish it…or why she hadn't stayed in a hotel when she'd been forced to vacate it. Why had she been so insistent on buying outright rather than taking a small mortgage or personal loan to leave her some working capital?

For now Jessica and the kittens were living with him. Having been alone for five years, he'd been nervous of her moving in but it felt scarily *right*. They fitted. As this was the first time he'd been attracted to another woman, he'd struggled with feelings of disloyalty. Something Sofia would chastise him for, having made it clear she didn't want him to remain alone.

Living with someone revealed so much about them and unearthed little ways and habits previously unsuspected and which could be irritating out of all proportion. So far he'd not discovered anything annoying about Jessica but there were several things that intrigued and amused him. One was the collection of assorted vitamin and dietary supplements she had stacked at one end of the kitchen worktop. He had no idea what they were for or why she felt she needed them. She was fastidious about washing up any of the crockery or cutlery she used, sorting them into a neat pile separate from his.

'Do you have a hygiene fetish?' he'd asked with a chuckle that first weekend, but his humour had rapidly faded given her reaction.

'No, of course not.'

The words of denial had been accompanied by a forced, hollow laugh, but it had been the unmistakeable hurt mixed with alarm and embarrassment in her eyes that had grabbed him.

'I didn't mean to upset you,' he'd apologised softly.

'You haven't.'

It had been a lie, he knew it. Just as he knew that something about what he had said or how he had said it had stung her.

The more he observed about her, including her anxiety at touching and being touched, the more he wondered if she'd experienced a bad relationship. Had someone criticised her, controlled her or, what he most feared, hurt and abused her?

Jess pivoted on one leg, turning her body in his direction, and he stifled a laugh when she spotted him, her eyes widening in surprise as she missed her step and stumbled momentarily before regaining her balance.

'Hi,' she murmured, embarrassment now predominant in her olive green eyes.

'Morning.' He straightened as she approached him warily, always keeping that extra bit of distance. 'Are you done?'

The fingers of one hand tucked stray wisps of hair back from her face. 'Just about. Why?'

'I have something to show you. Come with me.'

'Where are we going?' Jess asked as Gio drove away from the house.

'I can't tell you.'

She frowned at his unsatisfactory response. 'Why not?'

'Because then it would not be a surprise, would it?' he reasoned with calm amusement.

With no information forthcoming, Jess rested back in the luxurious seat of the sleek sports car. She hated to admit how much of a thrill she got each time she rode in it. As Gio turned out of the drive and onto the B-road that hugged the coastline on its route to St Piran, Jess glanced across the fields to the house she had been living in for the last fortnight. How could she feel so comfortable and yet scared at the same time?

The house sat atop the cliff as if carved from the bedrock and perfectly suited its Cornish name, *Ninnes*, 'the isolated place'. At first glance it suited Gio, too—wild, remote, alone.

'It's very impressive,' she'd murmured when she had first seen inside the architect-designed property. It didn't feel like a home. Clinical, cold, unlived in, it was like a set from an interior design magazine.

'Now tell me what you really think,' Gio had invited with a smile. 'It is soulless, no? A show-house, not a home,' he added, mirroring her own thoughts. 'The agent instructed to rent a place for me must have imagined someone moving from London would like it.'

'And you don't?' she'd asked, relieved this was not what he would have chosen for himself.

'No. But it gives me time to find something I *do* want and at least I have a roof over my head in the meantime.'

A laugh had burst from her at his unintentional choice of words and the expression on his face as the reason for her reaction dawned on him… she was there because she currently did *not* have a roof over hers!

Judging by the tone of his tirade when he had seen the state of her cottage, it had been worse than he'd expected. Had the property been in better condition, it would have been way beyond her budget, even with the unexpected legacy that had allowed her to step onto the housing ladder. But she had fallen in love with the place, and its parcel of neglected land that would allow her to have more animals and grow her own produce.

That Gio had seen the potential in the cottage had pleased her, and telling him about her plans for the place had diverted him from his questions about her reasons for not taking out a mortgage or personal loan. Either would have enabled her to get on with the renovations and furnishing the house straight away, but when she had looked into funding she had been asked questions about herself that she'd no wish to answer—and which may have meant she'd have been turned down anyway. She couldn't explain that to Gio without explaining *why*. And that was impossible.

So she had succumbed to Gio's arguments and the shameful temptation of moving in with him. Dickens and Kipling were in heaven. She was halfway between heaven and hell. They'd settled into a routine, their friendship becoming closer every day. Contrarily, his agreement to her rules and conditions had brought an inner stab of disappointment, though she knew friendship was all they could ever share.

Her hormones raged in protest, and she had to fight her attraction to him. Keeping people at a safe distance had become ingrained within her these last four years, but Gio was breaching her defences. He made her want things she could no longer have, reminding her of broken dreams and abandoned hopes.

'Jessica?'

'Mmm?' She blinked as Gio's voice impinged on her consciousness. 'Sorry, did you say something?'

He chuckled. 'Several times, but you are living

with goblins! That is the saying, yes?' he added as she stared at him blankly.

'Sorry?' she repeated, confused for a moment before realisation dawned. 'Oh! You mean away with the fairies! No, I was just thinking.' A flush warmed her cheeks. No way could she tell him where her thoughts had really been.

'We are here,' he said now, switching off the engine.

They were at the harbourside in St Piran, Jess discovered, scrambling out of the car before Gio could come round and offer a hand to help her. The less she touched him, the better. He took some things from the car, including a picnic basket, handing her a canvas bag with towels, spare T-shirts and some sunscreen. Apprehension unsettled her. She hadn't realised this was a day's outing.

Her gaze feasted on the sight of him dressed in deck shoes and shorts that left well-defined muscular legs bare from mid-thigh downwards. His torso was encased in a white T-shirt that emphasised the tone of his skin and hugged the contours of his athletic body. Jess bit her lip to stop a sigh of appreciation from escaping

'Have you been on a boat before?' he asked, guiding her towards a jetty along which several very expensive-looking craft were moored.

'Only a car ferry.'

His throaty laugh stole her breath. 'This isn't quite the same.'

Jess gathered that as he halted by a huge, gleaming, red-and-white speedboat. 'Oh, my.'

She gazed at the boat in awe, excitement mounting as she anticipated what it would feel like to ride in the kind of jet-powered boat she'd seen offshore racing on television. The name *Lori* was written on the side and she wondered at the significance.

'My one indulgence...apart from my car,' he told her with a touch of embarrassment.

'It's beautiful.' She smiled, imagining the thrill of speeding across the waves. 'How long have you had it?'

Relaxing, as if relieved at her reaction, he smiled the rare, special smile that reached his eyes, banishing the shadows that often lurked there and trapping the breath in her lungs. 'About eighteen months. I could not get out often when I was in London and she was moored on the south coast, but I hope to use her often here.'

Gio climbed aboard with practised ease, set down the items he was carrying and turned to help her. Jess swallowed. Adopting avoidance tactics, she gave him her bags instead of her hand.

'I can manage,' she told him, cursing the way he quirked an eyebrow and watched with amusement as she scrambled inelegantly over the side.

To her surprise, the luxury powerboat had a small but fully equipped cabin below, with a tiny kitchen, a minuscule washroom and a seating area that converted into a sleeping space for three people. They'd have to be very friendly, Jess thought. After putting the picnic items in the fridge, they went back outside and Gio collected two life-jackets from a locker.

'Are these necessary?' Jess asked as he handed one to her.

'Absolutely.' He fastened his in no time. 'I would never take risks with your safety.'

She knew that. They might not have known each other long but she trusted him implicitly. It was herself she worried about, she thought wryly as she struggled with the life-jacket, huffing with frustration as it defeated her.

'Here,' Gio chuckled, closing the gap between them. 'Let me help.'

'It's OK…'

Her protest fell on deaf ears as he took over. Did he need to touch her that much? Or so slowly and intimately? And he was far too close—so close that every breath she took was fragranced with his musky male scent, weakening her resolve and tightening the aching knot in the pit of her stomach. She couldn't stop breathing so she closed her eyes and tightened her hands into fists, praying for the exquisite torture to be over and reminding herself why she couldn't succumb to temptation. He was taking longer than necessary, surely, the brush of his fingers burning her through the fabric of her T-shirt.

'All done.'

His voice sounded huskier than usual and she opened her eyes to find herself staring directly into his. A tremor ran through her at the sensual expression he made no attempt to mask. Her body craved his touch, making it difficult for her to keep her distance, to step back now as she knew she must.

As if anticipating her retreat, he released her and moved away, but not before he dropped a kiss on the tip of her nose. Confused, Jess remained motionless for several moments. The tip of her nose felt warm and tingly...nothing to do with the late August heat and everything to do with the brush of his lips on her skin.

Why had he done that?

Why had she let him?

Panic welled within her. Maybe it would be best if she got off the boat now, before she did anything even more stupid. But while she was wrestling with indecision, considering her options, Gio effectively removed them by untying the moorings and firing the boat into life.

He settled her in the padded horseshoe-shaped seat adjacent to his, then he was manipulating the controls, inching the boat into the main harbour towards the open sea. The twin engines throbbed with leashed power, straining for freedom. Despite her uncertainties, a new burst of excitement coursed through her.

'I hate to confine your incredible hair, but you might want to tie it back—or I can lend you a baseball cap,' Gio said as the harbour entrance approached.

Taking his advice, she accepted the cap he offered, pulling her untamed curls back into a ponytail before feeding it through the slot in the back of the cap. The brim helped shade her eyes from the August sunshine.

'Hold on.'

Jess felt her heart thudding with excitement as they reached open water and gained speed, going west along the coast from St Piran. The sea was calm but the bow of the boat rose up and rode the crests and troughs. Gio opened the throttle and a whoop of joy escaped her. She felt free, truly understanding how he felt and how this blew away tensions and stresses.

'This is incredible!' She laughed, raising her

voice so Gio could hear her above the noise of the engines, the whoosh of the wind and the sound of the boat hitting the water. She tilted her head back and closed her eyes, savouring the sun on her skin, the occasional salty spray and the sense of speed. 'It's amazing! I love it.'

Lying face down on a towel stretched out on the sand in the secluded cove they had discovered, Jessica stretched and sighed. 'I could get used to this.'

Gio smiled. She sounded sleepy and contented following their exhilarating morning flying across the waves. They had travelled miles, moving from the bay in which St Piran stood, through Penhally Bay and past the village of Penhally itself, with its horseshoe-shaped harbour and the rocky promontory at one end, off which, Jessica had told him, lay the wreck of an old Spanish galleon.

They had headed part of the way back before finding their cove. After a swim, they had enjoyed their picnic lunch. As Jessica relaxed, he finished his apple, his gaze straying over her deliciously curvy figure. She had pulled her shorts on over her one-piece costume but that didn't spoil his view. Everything male in him responded to her voluptuous femininity. And her hair continued to captivate him. Freed from the cap, it seemed alive in the sunlight, the strands fanning across her shoulders like tongues of fire.

Her delight at the boat made Gio glad he'd brought her. He'd had doubts. He'd never taken anyone out with him before. Time on the boat was guarded jealously. It was his escape, his retreat, his guilty pleasure, and he'd been worried...not that Jessica wouldn't enjoy it but that having anyone with him would detract from what he gained being alone on the water. The desire for Jessica's company proved how fully she had breached his defences in the weeks since they'd met. Today he'd discovered that sharing the boat with her made the experience better than before.

'Why is your boat called *Lori*?'

Jessica's softly voiced question made him tense. She was looking at him through those sexy green eyes, and he dragged his gaze free, staring out to sea. Maybe it was time to tell her about Sofia. If he wanted Jessica to trust him and share the secrets that held her back from relationships with people, then he had to trust her, too. Which meant placing his broken heart in her hands. He cleared his throat, the emotion building before he even begun to speak.

'Lori was my wife's nickname,' he began, hit by a wave of memories. 'In Italy it is common to shorten someone's surname to use as a derivative. Sofia's maiden name was Loriani...to friends she was Lori. At school everyone called us "Lori and Cori".' A smile came unbidden. 'We used the names for each other into adulthood.'

Jessica's smile was sweet, interest and understanding in her eyes. 'That's lovely. You'd known each other a long time?'

'Since we were six.'

'Six?' she exclaimed with surprise. 'Wow!'

'Sofia's *mamma*, Ginetta, came to work for my parents,' he continued. 'She lived in, originally caring for the house—and me—while my parents worked long hours with the business.

Ginetta rapidly became indispensable, and she and Sofia were soon part of the family.'

Gio paused and took a drink of water. 'Sofia and I were the same age and were friends from day one. We scarcely spent a day apart. Many people believed we'd go our separate ways with time, but it never happened. It wasn't something we planned.' He frowned, trying to find the best way to explain. 'We just never wanted anyone else, you know?' Jessica nodded and turned more towards him. 'We married at eighteen. I did my medical training and Sofia trained to be a teacher. Throughout everything we remained best friends.'

'Soul mates,' Jessica added, her voice husky.

'Yes.'

Leaning back on his elbows, enjoying the feel of the sun against his skin, he found himself telling her all kinds of stories as happy memories flowed so quickly it was difficult to catch hold of them.

'We were in no hurry to start a family of our own. Being together was all we wanted. We thought we had time...but it ran out,' he added, choking on the words.

'What happened, Gio?'

Jessica's whispered query took him back into the darkness. Voice thick, he told her of the moment they had found out that Sofia was dying.

'It is ironic, no, that Sofia should be struck down by the kind of brain tumour I now operate on often?' He heard Jessica's shocked gasp, aware that she was sitting up but too lost in his thoughts to stop now. 'Sofia's tumour was inoperable. It was virulent and resistant to treatment, claiming her quickly.'

What he didn't add aloud was how guilty he felt. And that he couldn't forgive himself for being unable to save her, tormenting himself as he relived those terrible weeks...to the signs he must have missed and failing to catch the tumour early enough to make a difference. His head knew it wasn't true, Sofia's doctors had told him time and again that it wouldn't have made a difference, but still he wondered and beat himself up over his failings.

'Gio, you're not in any way to blame.' Jessica was closer, he could feel her behind him, feel the kiss of her breath against his shoulder as she spoke, her voice gentle but firm. He heard the emotion she was keeping in check as she continued. 'It is too unspeakably cruel, for Sofia and for you.'

'I wish I had her courage. She faced death with the same warmth, bravery, humour and gentleness of spirit with which she embraced life. I was at her side every second of her brief but futile fight, and I was holding her hand when she took her final breath.'

His colleagues and the staff who had cared for her had left him alone with her. For the first time in his adult life, he had wept—for Sofia and for himself. And then he had shut down a significant part of himself, closing off his heart because it was the only way he could cope with going on alone. As he had somehow emerged from the blackest of days after her loss, he had thrown himself into his work, into making himself better, and in trying to stop others dying the way Sofia had.

'Life was nothing without her. We'd been inseparable for twenty-one years. I felt lost, cast adrift,' he admitted, the emotion catching up with him.

'Gio...'

Jessica came up onto her knees behind him and wrapped him in her arms, shocking him. Full, firm breasts pressed against his back and, as she rested her head on his shoulder, he felt her tears against his skin. As he drew in another unsteady breath, it was fragranced with the subtle aroma of her chocolate-scented shampoo and body lotion. Drawing on her comfort, he raised his hands, finding hers and linking their fingers.

'You worked so you wouldn't think,' she said, her voice throaty with emotion.

'Yes.' She understood, he suspected, because she did the same, focusing on other people's problems to escape her own.

'And the trust you told me about...'

'I set it up in Sofia's name, funding research, raising money to provide scanners and equipment for hospitals around the world and providing information and support for those struck down by neurological conditions, especially tumours.'

'Sofia would be so proud of you.'

'She would also be kicking me for not getting on with life,' he added wryly.

'But you have,' Jessica protested. 'You did what you needed to do for you and you've helped countless others through very difficult times.'

Her generosity touched him. And he savoured the closeness and physical contact, hoping Jessica would not suddenly remember her no-touching rule and take flight.

He took a deep breath, feeling calmer, telling Jessica of his discovery of the album Sofia had made of their lives, packed with photos and letters and memorabilia from childhood, through their wedding and to their last days together. He treasured it. It gave him solace, made him grateful that she'd been his life, but it also made him grieve for what would never be. Sofia was the only woman he had ever loved, the only woman with whom he had ever *made* love. In the last five years his bed had felt too big and cold and lonely, but nothing and no one had ever tempted him.

Until Jessica.

As Gio fell silent, Jess thought over all he had told her, feeling devastated for him and his wife. Many times she had wondered about the woman who had claimed Gio's heart. Sofia. She envisaged a glamorous, beautiful woman with a model-like figure. Whatever she had looked like, Sofia had been lucky to win Gio's love, devotion and loyalty. And cruelly unlucky to have been taken from him at such a young age.

Gio's fidelity and love for Sofia was in stark contrast to the thoughtlessness and infidelity shown by Duncan, Jess's ex-fiancé and the man who had changed her life for ever. Discovering Duncan had been unfaithful on too many occasions to count had been hurtful and shocking enough. Being eight weeks away from the wedding she had dreamed of for so long had made it worse. The wedding had never taken place. And the dream would now never come true for her.

There were so many things Duncan had taken

from her, including her trust in people. And herself. Her life had changed beyond recognition. Her fiancé—*ex-fiancé*, she corrected with the anger and bitterness that had never left her—had seen to that.

The thought of never being close to anyone again was depressing, so she kept busy and absorbed helping others so that she had no time to think of herself. So she understood Gio's need to lose himself in work after such a heart-wrenching loss. That he blamed himself was terrible, and yet driving himself as he had meant he had given hope, care and fresh chances to his patients. Patients he tried so hard to save as he had not been able to save Sofia.

Her situation was different but the outcome had been similar. A lonely life devoting herself to caring for others. Now and again, in a weak moment, a stray thought crept in. A yearning for intimacy. Not even sex…just a need to be held and cherished. As she and Gio were holding each other now.

The reality of it was a shock. She'd acted on instinct in response to his pain, forgetting the need to keep distance between them. Now, pressed against him, her arms around his shoulders and their hands locked together, she battled the awareness and desire that were coursing through her.

How she wished she could satisfy the urge to bury her face more fully into his neck and breathe in his scent…the earthy aroma of man mixed with the subtle but arousing fragrance of his soap and warm, sun-kissed skin. It was crazy! But everything in her was drawn to him on some basic level. She couldn't give in to it. To do so would involve telling him her secrets and she couldn't do that. If she did, he would run in the opposite direction, just as everyone else in her life had done when they'd found out. She was tarnished, spoiled goods, untouchable. And she would do well to remember that when she indulged in any foolish notions about Gio.

Drawing in one last breath of his intoxicating, delicious scent, her desire for him threatening to melt her bones and turn her resolve to dust, she began to withdraw.

'I'm sorry, I shouldn't have done that,' she apologised, disconcerted when he kept hold of her hands.

'I'm not sorry.' He allowed her to place only a small distance between them before shifting so he was facing her. 'Thank you.'

Jess shook her head in confusion. 'I didn't do anything.'

'Yes, you did. You listened, you understood. You cared,' he added huskily, setting her heart thudding.

Knowing she was in big trouble, Jess sucked in a ragged breath, unable to drag her gaze free from the intensity of his. 'W-what are you look-ing at?' she finally asked, the electric tension increasing with every passing second.

'Your eyes.'

Jess frowned. 'What's the matter with them?'

'Nothing. They're beautiful.' He smiled, seem-ing closer than ever. 'This is the first time I've noticed the little specks of silver-grey in them.'

'Really?' Was that her voice sounding so breathless and confused?

'Mmm.' Blue eyes darkened as they watched

her. 'I've meant to ask before…what is the gem-stone in your earrings? They're the same shade as your eyes.'

Again he had thrown her and she tried to focus on his question and not on the affect of his near-ness. 'Olive apatite. My grandmother had a pas-sion for gemology and she gave them to me for my twenty-first birthday,' she told him, think-ing with sadness and gratitude of the woman who had died the previous winter and whose unexpected legacy had enabled her to buy her cottage.

'They're perfect for you,' Gio told her, the ap-proval and intimacy in his voice making her tingle all over.

Jess couldn't help but shiver as Gio ran the pad of one thumb along the sensitive hollow be-tween her chin and her lower lip. She couldn't prevent her lips parting in response. It took a con-certed effort not to sway towards him. Instead, Gio moved, oh, so slowly leaning in until warm supple lips met hers. Jess jumped. One of his hands still held hers and her fingers closed re-flexively on his.

He tasted of things sinful, things long denied her but which she could know again if only she let go. Could she? Dared she? What if she did? How would she put the lid back on the box again afterwards? More than anything she wanted to forget common sense.

But she couldn't.

Gathering all the strength and willpower she could muster, she turned her head away, breaking the spell. She heard his soft sigh, his smothered exclamation of regret and frustration, but she hardened her resolve. It was for the best, she told herself over and over again, hoping that repeating the mantra often enough would make her believe it. But the thought of telling him the truth made it easier.

The truth.

Her secret.

The one that hung over her like the sword of Damocles. Nothing could happen without him knowing—and once he knew, he would reject her anyway. Like everyone else. She valued his friendship too much to risk spoiling everything by giving in to a moment of madness, one she knew had no future to it.

'Jessica…'

'Please, Gio, don't,' she begged before he could continue. 'I can't. I'm sorry.'

His disappointment was clear, but he smiled, running one finger down her cheek. 'It's OK. I'm not giving up on you but there is no hurry. When you are ready, you will tell me…whatever it is.'

Jess had no reply to that, unable to imagine a time when she could ever reveal the truth to him.

'Friends, remember?' she said now, moving away and helping him pack their things ready to return to the boat for the journey home.

She'd told Gio to remember the rules, but she had been as guilty as him of ignoring them. With the boundaries becoming more and more blurred all the time, who most needed the instruction to behave…Gio or herself?

CHAPTER SEVEN

'MEGAN?'

Josh O'Hara looked at the fragile form of the woman who had caused much of the mental and emotional turmoil that had plagued him since he'd arrived at St Piran's and discovered her here. A blast from the past. One with which he'd never come to terms.

She turned around, her gaze scanning the A and E staffroom, and a frown formed as she realised they were alone. He felt uncertain and awkward as the silence stretched between them. They had been tiptoeing around each other for weeks now. He had questions that needed answers, but attempts to confront the past had been futile…meeting with hostility and denial.

Yet despite the dark cloud that hung over them, when Megan, as registrar on call, had come to A and E from Paediatrics, they'd worked well together and been attuned to each other. Now he had a rare window of opportunity to talk to her alone.

'Have you been in Cornwall all the time?' he asked, daring to venture onto dangerous ground.

Her gaze flicked to his and away again. 'Pretty much.'

At least she'd answered rather than walking out or telling him to back off. 'How is your grandmother?'

'She died three years ago.'

'I'm sorry.' Damn it, could he say nothing right to this woman? 'I know what she meant to you.'

Her small smile was tinged with sadness. 'I owe her everything.'

She'd told him once how her parents had been killed in a road accident when she'd been four and her grandmother had raised her. She'd not been in the best of health and Megan had been caring for her while going through medical school.

With Megan in a more conciliatory mood, he

risked asking more of the questions that plagued him. 'Why here, Megan?'

'My grandmother lived in Penhally when she was young and she wanted to come home before she died. It seemed as good a place as any to be,' she finished, sounding so lost and alone that his heart ached for her.

He'd forgotten her grandmother's connection with Cornwall. Or had he? Was that why, when Rebecca had suggested leaving London, Cornwall had been the first place he had thought to go? Had he, some place deep in his subconscious, made the connection with Megan?

He remained as affected by her as he'd always been. The past would never go away. Neither could he change it. But he craved answers.

'I know you don't want to talk, and I won't ask again if that's what you choose, but I need to know, Megan—' He broke off, capturing her gaze, his heart in his mouth. 'Was the baby mine?'

He saw her shock and the pain his question caused as she reeled back, anger replacing the hurt in her eyes. 'Of *course* it was yours.

Don't judge me by *your* standards. *I* didn't sleep around.'

'Why didn't you *tell* me?' he demanded, his own hurt and anger rising with the confirmation of what he had known in his heart all along.

'How could I?' she threw back at him, her voice shaky with emotion. 'When was I meant to tell you? You refused to talk to me. And what good would it have done? What would *you* have done? You'd made it clear I meant nothing to you. You wouldn't have welcomed fatherhood… you never wanted children. Just as you rejected marriage—although *that's* changed in the last eight years.'

Pain and bitterness rang in her tone. Her accusations hurt…the more so because he recognised the truth in them. He *had* behaved badly. He'd been anti-marriage—for himself—and he'd never wanted children. Something he'd made clear to Rebecca from the first, and the reason why he was refusing her latest demands for a baby.

But he didn't want to think of Rebecca now. His thoughts were in the past. He'd had a right to know eight years ago. Hadn't he? Megan's challenge rang in his ears. What *would* he have done? He wasn't sure but it would undoubtedly have been the wrong thing. Avoidance of the truth. Running away. He'd been good at that. But knowing it *had* been his lifeless son he'd once held in his arms was devastating.

'You denied me any chance of making those decisions for myself.' The depth of his emotion shocked him and his voice was choked. 'You gave me no chance to say goodbye to my son.'

'You have a nerve. What chance did *you* give *me* when you tossed me aside?' Tears gleamed on her lashes. 'You took my baby from me, Josh. And with him any chance of me having another child.'

'God, Megan. Those weren't my decisions.' His tone softened as her pain sliced through him. She looked more fragile than ever and he fought the urge to comfort her—something he should have done eight years ago.

Eight years…

He was plunged back to that terrible night when A and E had been in chaos following a multiple crash involving a coach of schoolchildren. He'd been a junior doctor facing something far beyond his experience as the paramedics had brought in a woman in the throes of a miscarriage and haemorrhaging terribly. Discovering it was Megan had thrown him.

'The obstetrician/gynaecologist did what was necessary to save your life. There wasn't even time to transfer you to Theatre.'

The possibility of Megan dying had been real. The surgeon had pulled the tiny baby from her body and given it to him. He'd stared at the lifeless form, too premature to survive, trying to work out dates with a brain that refused to function. A nurse had taken the baby away, and he'd been drawn back into the emergency procedure, assisting as the surgeon had made the decision to take Megan's womb.

'I asked him—*begged* him—to leave you hope for the future, but he was adamant there was no other way to stop you bleeding to death. What else could I have done?' he appealed to her, his stomach churning as he relived that awful night.

'I don't know.'

Tears ran down her cheeks and his heart, for so long encased in a protective coating of stone, threatened to break at the depth of her sorrow and pain. He'd pushed the memories into the background, unable to deal with them. Megan had been living with them every day. He felt guilty, confused...

'What did you call him?' he asked, knowing he was tormenting them both but needing to know.

'Stephen.' Her voice was rough. 'After my father.'

'Thank you for telling me.'

They stared at each other, fighting the past, the pain, the memories—and the chemistry that, eight years on and despite all that had happened, still bubbled below the surface.

The sound of his pager announcing an incoming emergency cut through the tense silence, swiftly followed by the ring of Megan's pager, bringing their conversation to an end. Although he now had confirmation about the baby, a sense of unfinished business still remained.

Eight years ago he had known that Megan was

different, had sensed she was dangerous to him. And he'd been right. The night he'd let down his guard had been the most amazing of his life. He'd told Megan things he had never told anyone else, and she had touched a place inside him in a way no other woman ever had. It had scared him. And he'd done what Megan had accused him of. He'd blanked her, keeping as far from her as possible because she'd burrowed under his skin.

If only he had been mature enough to know what he knew now. That the sort of connection he had found with Megan was rare. Not just the incredible physical passion that had over-whelmed them both but the deep mental and emotional union he'd experienced with no one but her. By the time he'd realised what he could have had and all he had thrown away, it had been too late.

He'd wobbled. Briefly. Then he'd gone on, focusing on his career and rapid advancement. Four years ago he'd met Rebecca and they'd seemed to want the same things, including no children. He'd cared about her, he'd been lonely and enjoyed having her to come home to. She'd wanted the doctor husband and the lifestyle. He'd convinced himself it was for the best, not the same as he'd had with Megan but safer.

Things had been wrong long before they'd left London. Bored, Rebecca had changed the rules, deciding she wanted a child. But as Izzy had said weeks ago when her daughter had been born, a child couldn't hold a bad marriage together and shouldn't be brought into the world for the wrong reasons. He wouldn't have a baby he didn't want with a woman he didn't love and who didn't love him.

Seeing Megan again, he saw with terrible clarity what he had thrown away, and he wished with all his heart that he had done things differently when he'd had the chance. As they walked down the corridor to the main A and E department, it occurred to him that he had still not asked Megan one of the questions that had been bugging him all along.

'Why *did* you stay the night with me, Megan?'

Her sharp intake of breath was audible, but she pushed through the swing doors into the busy department, bringing further discussion to an end. As he was directed to Resus, Megan was called to a treatment cubicle and she walked away from him without a backward glance. He had no more idea what to do about her—and his feelings for her—now than he had in the past. She was an itch under his skin that wouldn't go away, affecting him in the same unique way she had done eight years ago.

'Is there anything else I can do for you?' Jess asked, sitting beside the bed of the woman with whom she had spent a considerable amount of time over the last few days.

Faye Luxton, in her early seventies, had come in for a standard knee replacement but had suffered a severe bleed in her brain during her operation and had woken in Intensive Care to find her world turned upside down. She'd been handed over into Gio's care and, just days ago, he had needed to operate on a second bleed to remove a clot and also to put a coil around a small aneurysm that had threatened to enlarge and cause even greater problems.

Unfortunately, the damage already caused could not be reversed, although the numbness and weakness down one side of her body and her difficulty speaking were improving. Faye could still have a good quality of life, but she would no longer be able to live alone or care for herself and her animals.

With no family, Faye faced the horrible necessity of selling her much-loved home and moving into an assisted-care facility. Jess had helped support her when Social Services had come to discuss the options.

Faye had faced everything with courage, but had been distressed at times as she tried to come to terms with the drastic changes in her life. Jess had done all she could, helping Faye deal with the emotional upset.

'You've done so much.' Her speech was slow and slurred, but clearer than it had been. 'I wouldn't have coped without you.'

'I'm sure you would. You have such a strong spirit, Faye. You've been a joy to care for and a real inspiration, too,' Jess assured her.

'I agree.'

Gio's voice sent a prickle of awareness along Jess's spine and she looked round, her gaze clashing with his as he strode through the door, his senior registrar, a couple of junior doctors and the ward's charge nurse trailing in his wake. Jess was all too conscious of Gio close beside her chair, blocking her exit, his leg and hip pressing gently against her, as he greeted Faye warmly.

'I'll step out,' Jess offered, making to rise.

'Can Jess stay?' Faye asked, looking unsettled.

Gio smiled at their patient. 'Yes, of course.'

Jess subsided back onto the chair as his hand came to rest on her shoulder. Although his attention was focused on the medical team updating him on Faye's condition, his hand lingered, and Jess felt the fire in her blood as his touch warmed her through the fabric of her shirt. His fingers gave a gentle squeeze before he released her and reached out for Faye's notes.

They were halfway through September and while they'd been on their best behaviour since their bank-holiday outing in the boat, Jess was finding it difficult to ignore the electric buzz of attraction that intensified with every passing day. But she valued their friendship too much to risk losing her head and doing anything stupid.

They'd been out on the boat twice more and she loved it. Much to her amazement, Gio had also been teaching her how to drive it. The thrill had been so huge it had even managed to take her mind off his body pressed close to hers—and the divine male scent of him—as he'd helped her work the controls.

The tragedy of his wife's death still affected her and she remained shocked at the way she had acted on instinct in response to his grief. It had scared her. With Gio it was too easy to forget the hard lessons of the last four years.

Curious, Jess had steeled herself to ask Gio more about Sofia a couple of nights ago. Gio had brought out the album Sofia had made when she'd known she was dying, creating a story of their lives in words and pictures, and Jess had choked up all over again at the incredible bond they had shared and the cruel way they had been parted.

Sofia had been a surprise. Rather than being

model thin and styled to perfection, she'd been small, curvy and very much the girl next door, possessing the kind of fresh-faced natural beauty that could never be faked and that shone through because of the person she was, in her laughing dark eyes, her smile and her obvious love for Gio. And his for her.

The photos of Gio and Sofia in their teens, so much together, so right for each other and so in love, had reminded Jess of Marcia and Colin— another young couple who had been ripped apart by terrible tragedy, and one she hadn't been able to get out of her mind.

'How are you feeling, Faye?' Gio asked, sitting on the edge of the bed and taking her good hand in his.

'I'm frustrated my body won't do what I want it to. I can't even tell you properly.' Faye shook her head. 'I can't imagine life away from my home and without my animals. I'm thankful for all you've done for me, but knowing things will never be the same is difficult.'

'Of course. It's hard enough to recover from surgery without having to come to terms with such unexpected changes. Things seem over-whelming, yes?' he sympathised, stealing Jess's heart as he took a pristine handkerchief from his pocket and wiped the elderly lady's tears with gentle care.

'Yes, exactly.' Faye visibly relaxed, soothed by Gio's attention. 'I'm old and set in my ways.'

Gio gallantly protested, making her smile. 'You're doing well and we will all do everything we can to ensure you regain as much strength and capability as possible.' The air locked in Jess's lungs as his gaze flicked to her. 'Jessica is here to help make the transition as trouble-free as possible.'

'I'm so worried about my animals, but Jess is marvellous,' Faye confided to Gio. 'If other ar-rangements can't be made to keep them together, she's promised she'll care for them herself.'

A blush warmed Jess's cheeks as Gio looked at her, his expression unreadable.

Gio talked with Faye awhile longer before rising to his feet. His entourage exited ahead of him but he lingered, and Jess excused herself from Faye, worried about his reaction to the animal thing.

'I was going to tell you, Gio. The workmen are making good progress on the cottage, and I'll arrange to have the fences dealt with. If the animals have to be moved before I'm back home, I'll ask Flora if she has room for them until I'm ready,' she rushed to reassure him. 'I don't expect you to house them or anything. I—'

Her rushed words were silenced as Gio pressed a finger to her lips. 'Stop apologising.' Blue eyes twinkled with amusement and something else she couldn't discern but which made her warm and tingly and a little bit scared. 'I would have been surprised had you *not* offered to step in.'

'Oh…'

He glanced each way along the corridor, his tone conspiratorial as he leaned closer to her, making her quiver with awareness as his warm breath fanned her face. 'Shall I tell you a secret?'

She nodded, unable to answer, hardly able to breathe, fighting every urge within her to touch him, hug him, kiss him.

'I was going to make the same pledge to Faye myself.'

Jess blinked, his nearness robbing her of thought. 'You were?'

'I was.'

Jess felt mesmerised, her skin aflame as he ran one finger down her cheek. The suddenness of an alarm further along the corridor had her snapping back, conscious of where they were. Disconcerted by his touch, she stepped away. There was nothing she could do to escape the non-physical connection, the electrically charged one that bound her ever more tightly to him.

Gio's hand slowly dropped to his side and she swallowed as she met his gaze. He smiled, the full-on smile that stole her breath. 'I must go,' he said, glancing at his watch. 'We'll drive out to Faye's after work to talk with her neighbour and decide what is best to be done. OK?'

'OK.'

Jess watched as he strode off to join his team. How was she going to cope when she moved back to her own cottage with the kittens? Gio had become far too important in her life.

'Stop the car!'

Gio reacted instantly to Jessica's cry, startled

when she opened the door and scrambled out before they'd come to a stop. Cursing in Italian, he parked safely at the side of the road and climbed out in time to see Jessica running along the pavement and disappearing from view around a corner. Concerned, Gio jogged after her. What was earth going on?

They were in the centre of St Piran, on the way home following their visit to Faye's small-holding. Enquiries to several rescue centres had proved futile, which left them bemused and amused to find themselves foster-parents to a motley collection of animals. There were more than Gio had anticipated. He'd wanted animals, yes, but he hadn't imagined taking on so many in one go! Jessica's enthusiasm had swayed him, though.

Now, along with Dickens and Kipling, their menagerie included a donkey, two Gloucester Old Spot pigs, three sheep of mixed heritage and several assorted chickens. Faye's neighbour would care for them in the short term until the fencing at Jessica's cottage, and the necessary movement licences, were arranged. Gio didn't want to think about Jessica moving out—he had ideas but it was too soon to discuss them—but whatever happened between Jessica and himself, he intended to share the cost and responsibility for the animals.

Rounding the corner, he saw Jessica walking back towards him, her shoulders slumped, her steps reluctant as she kept pausing and looking behind her.

'What's going on?' he asked as he joined her.

She looked up, olive-green eyes despondent. 'I saw Marcia.' Again she scanned the crowds along one of St Piran's main shopping streets.

'The girl who gave you the false name after her boyfriend died?' he asked, frowning at her nod of confirmation. 'Are you still fretting about her?'

'Yes.'

She tried to carry everyone's problems on her own shoulders. 'Jessica...'

'I saw her, Gio. She looked so alone, so lost. The girl I met was prettily plump and well groomed,' she told him, clearly upset. 'She's put on weight and hasn't been taking care of herself. Her skin was grey and her hair lank and unstyled.' Again she met his gaze, and his chest tightened at the expression in her eyes. 'I can't help but worry about her.'

'You have a special empathy with people. But you can't solve everyone's problems, *fiamma*,' he advised her, the endearment—meaning flame in Italian—slipping out without conscious thought.

'I know that, but—'

As her defensive words snapped off, Gio cupped her face. 'Marcia knows where you are. If she needs you, she'll contact you in her own time. Everyone comes to terms with grief in their own way. Believe me, I know.'

Fresh tears stung Jessica's eyes as Gio's words hit home, pain for him mingling with her anxiety for Marcia. 'I'm sorry.'

'There's nothing to apologise for.' His smile was gentle, as was his touch.

Jess bit her lip, fighting the temptation, the *need*, to step closer, to press herself against him and be hugged…held in those strong arms. 'I'm OK,' she lied, stepping back and manufacturing a smile.

'Jess!' A female voice called her name and she looked round, smiling as she saw Kate Althorp approaching. 'Hello, my love.'

'Hi, Kate, how are you? And how is Jem?' She had spent many an hour talking with the older woman, especially when her son had been badly hurt in a car accident earlier in the year.

Kate's smile was free from the shadows Jess had seen there in the past. 'Jem's made a wonder-ful recovery. Thank you. And we're all well.'

'I'm so glad.' She was painfully conscious of Gio beside her and, when Kate looked at him expectantly, Jess had to introduce them. 'Kate, this is Gio Corezzi. He's a neurosurgeon and joined St Piran's in August,' she explained, her gaze flicking to him and away again. 'Gio, meet Kate Althorp. She's a midwife at the surgery in Penhally.'

Jess watched as the two shook hands and ex-changed pleasantries, noting how Kate glowed when faced with Gio's natural charm and humour.

'What Jess has modestly left out, Gio, is how wonderful she has been to me,' Kate told him. 'She not only helped me a year ago when I had a scary brush with breast cancer, but she was an absolute rock when my son, Jem, broke his pelvis five months ago.'

'I didn't really do anything,' Jess murmured with embarrassment.

Kate waved her protest aside. 'What nonsense! I couldn't have got through it all without you, life was so difficult,' the older woman insisted, deepening Jess's blush and her discomfort. Kate smiled up at Gio. 'Jess is one in a million.'

'Yes…I know.'

Jess opened her mouth then closed it again, unsure what to say in response to Gio's husky words.

Kate chuckled, a twinkle in her brown eyes. She glanced at her watch and sighed. 'I'm afraid I have to run. There's so little time before the wedding and I have a million things to do. You are coming, aren't you, my love? I so want you to be there, it would mean so much to me. Bring Gio,' she added with a wink.

As Kate hurried off, Jess turned to walk back towards the car, but Gio surprised her, catching her hand and leading her in the opposite direction. 'This way.'

'Where are we going?' she asked, all too conscious of the way her fingers curled naturally with his.

'You're going to need a dress for the wedding and, as Kate said, there isn't much time.' He headed in the direction of one of St Piran's classy boutiques. 'We can take care of it while we are here.'

Jessica tried to dig her heels in. No way could she afford anything from that kind of shop. 'I'm not sure if I'm going to go,' she admitted, pulling on his hand.

'Not go?' He halted, an eyebrow raised in query as he looked at her. 'Why ever not?'

She attempted a careless shrug. He'd known about the wedding—the invitation had been propped on the mantelpiece in his living room for some time—but now he'd met Kate, it was more difficult to explain. It was one thing inter-acting with Kate at the hospital and quite an-other to move things into a social context. Jess didn't do social. Telling Gio that she felt too shy and nervous to go to the wedding on her own sounded far too pathetic.

'Kate wants you to be there,' he pointed out.

'Yes, but—'

'But nothing.' Gio forestalled further protests, the smile that curved his sexy mouth doing pe-culiar things to her insides.

'Gio,' she protested as he started them walking again.

'I'm going to buy you a frock for the wedding, to which I shall be honoured to escort you,' he informed her, shock rendering her temporarily compliant as he guided her along and halted out-side the door of the boutique.

'Gio, you can't buy me a dress!'

'Of course I can!' He tweaked the tip of her nose between finger and thumb of his free hand.

Gazing at him in confusion, her skin tingling from his touch, she swallowed, all too conscious that this man was getting far too close. The walls she had constructed for her own protection felt increasingly vulnerable. And she was scared. Scared that if she continued to allow Gio to breach her defences and become more than a platonic friend, she would end up breaking her heart all over again.

And this time she might never recover.

CHAPTER EIGHT

IT WAS wonderful to see Kate so happy. Sitting with Polly d'Azzaro and a heavily pregnant Lucy Carter, in the garden of the beautiful granite-built barn a few miles outside Penhally that was now Kate's home, Jess watched the older woman mingle with her guests. She had a broad smile on her face, her brown eyes were alight with joy, and Nick, her new husband, was never far from her side.

St Mark's, Penhally's small church, had been bursting at the seams as people had come from far and wide to attend Nick and Kate's wedding. Nick's grown-up children from his first marriage had been there to support their father and give their blessing to Kate. And Kate's eleven-year-old son Jem, who had only recently discovered that Nick was his real father, had recovered well enough from his broken pelvis to proudly walk his mother down the aisle. A lump had formed in Jess's throat as Jem had stood with his half-brothers and -sister, watching his mother marry his father, publicly acknowledging him and making them one big united family at last.

Nervous about attending the party, Jess would never have come alone. Having Gio there made her feel better. When they'd arrived at the barn, anxiety had gripped her as she'd faced the prospect of socialising with so many people. Unconsciously she'd moved closer to Gio. A moment later her right hand had been enveloped in his left one. Far from flinching away, or re-minding him of the no-touching rule, her fingers had linked with his and held on tight.

Now, several hours later, after endless chat and laughter, an informal buffet, complete with hog roast and lashings of champagne, the dancing was soon to begin. Having enjoyed things more than she'd expected to—although she'd lost count of the number of times she'd explained she and Gio were just friends—the prospect of the live band and dancing into the evening was making her tense.

Jess's gaze strayed to Gio, who was deep in conversation with Polly's husband, Luca. Both Italian and with similar tragedies in their pasts, the two men had much in common. Luca was also Jess's GP.

'Gio's very handsome,' Polly commented, following the direction of her gaze.

'Mmm.' Jess hoped her murmur of agreement sounded noncommittal, even though her heart did somersaults every time she looked at him. He was always stunning but in his suit and tie he looked like a matinée idol. 'We're just friends.'

Polly's blue eyes were filled with understanding. 'That's a shame.'

'It's for the best.' Jess's words emerged as a whisper and, however much she wanted to deny it, even she could hear the regret in her voice.

'Is it?' Polly's smile was kind. As a fellow GP at Penhally surgery, Jess knew the other woman was speaking both as a doctor and a woman. 'Are you sure, Jess?'

She nodded, glancing at Polly before her gaze was drawn inexorably back to Gio. 'Yes.'

Although it was getting harder and harder to believe it.

Before Polly could say any more, Nick and Kate passed on their way indoors to prepare for the first dance. Nick looked on with an indulgent and contented smile as Kate hugged Polly, whom, Jess had discovered, was Kate's god-daughter.

'We're so glad you and Gio came, Jess, and thank you so much for your lovely gift and the beautiful words in your card,' Kate told her, linking her arm through Nick's. 'You're looking gorgeous today.'

'Thank you,' Jess murmured, taken by surprise.

She was wearing the dress Gio had insisted on buying at the boutique in St Piran. Sleeveless and deceptively simple, it fell to her knees, highlighting her curves, the shades of teal and peacock green bringing out the colour of her eyes and highlighting the rich reds in her hair, now drawn back in a ponytail. She felt guilty for giving in to temptation—and Gio's persuasion—but the instant she had put the expensive dress on, she'd fallen in love with it. The desire and appreciation in Gio's eyes when he'd seen her in it had set her blood zinging in her veins.

'Enjoy yourselves,' Nick instructed with a benevolent smile before leading Kate away.

Gio and Luca returned, bringing non-alcoholic fruit punch with them, which both she and Polly accepted gratefully. She met Gio's gaze, her stomach muscles tightening at the expression in his intense blue eyes, her hand not entirely steady as she sipped the ice-cold drink.

Jess was about to tell Gio that she'd like to leave before the dancing began when Luca's twin daughters came running towards them. She'd been shocked when she'd heard how their mother had died giving birth to them. Now four and a half, they were adorable, so alike in looks but so different in character. It was the bolder, more outgoing Toni who arrived first.

'Mummy Polly?' she asked breathlessly.

'Yes, darling?'

'Rosie wants to know if she can have more cake.'

'Does she?' Jess saw Polly's lips twitch as she

saw through the ruse. 'You can tell Rosie she can have a piece if she wants one.'

Toni's eyes widened and her mouth formed a silent O as she realised what had happened and tried to work out what to do about it. Gio and Luca both chuckled. Toni glanced round at her sister and then looked pleadingly up at her father, who hid his grin by taking a drink. The little girl's anxious gaze returned to Polly.

'Would *you* like another piece of cake, too, Toni?' she queried, unable to contain her amusement.

'Yes, please!' The relief on the child's face was so funny they all laughed.

'All right,' Polly agreed. 'You can both have one more *small* piece each.'

The little girl leaned in and kissed her step-mother soundly on the cheek. 'Thank you!'

As Toni ran off to join her quieter sister, Jess experienced for the first time the pressing weight of regret that she would never know the joy of motherhood. She hadn't thought of it much before. She'd never felt a maternal yearning, neither had she and Duncan ever discussed having a family.

Now, seeing the twins, she couldn't help but wonder what Gio's children would look like… although any idea of *her* ever being with him was pure fantasy. But it hit home that this was one more thing Duncan had taken away from her.

Gio was aware of the change in Jessica but was unsure of its cause. She put on a smiling face, but a light had dimmed in her eyes. He wanted to know what had happened. Unfortunately this was neither the time nor the place to ask. He was proud of her. She'd been nervous and uncomfortable about the party, even before she had clung so tenaciously to his hand when faced with the throng of guests. But she'd gradually relaxed, especially when the d'Azzaro family had taken them under their collective wings.

He'd enjoyed himself, too. Much of that had been simply being with Jessica, but he'd also been pleased to meet Luca. Discovering that Luca's life had mirrored his own in many ways had given him much to think about, especially seeing how Luca had been able to move on to find love and happiness with Polly.

'It wasn't easy,' Luca had told him. 'For so long I lived only for my girls. I'd not even looked at anyone else after Elaine died and I never expected to love again. Then I met Polly.' His smile and tone of voice had revealed his emotion more than words. 'I'm so lucky. And grateful. Don't close your heart and mind to possibilities, Gio,' he'd advised, his dark gaze straying to where Jessica and Polly had been sitting. 'You have the chance for something special. Jess deserves the best. She's not someone to be toyed with.'

The warning had been gently given, but it was a warning nonetheless. Luca and Polly not only viewed Jessica with affection, they were also protective of her. Gio wondered what his compatriot knew but was unable to reveal because of patient confidentiality.

After the live band struck up, Nick and Kate taking the first dance, most of the guests took to the floor. Jessica, however, refused all offers. It was Luca who eventually managed to get her on her feet, and Gio was shocked by the rush of

envy and possessiveness that washed over him.
Luca was happily married and had no designs
on Jessica, but Gio hated to see her in anyone's
arms but his own.

'Would you mind dancing with me, Gio?'

Polly's request took him by surprise. 'I'd be
delighted,' he agreed politely, although the only
person he wanted was Jessica.

'Don't worry, it won't be for long.' Polly, a
pretty blonde and tiny, smiled up at him. 'Luca's
giving Jess a pep talk.'

'A pep talk?' Gio frowned. What was Luca
saying to her? And why?

Polly glanced across to where her husband
and Jessica were dancing. 'Be ready to take over
when Luca gives the signal.'

Puzzled but intrigued, Gio did as he was
bidden, eager for the moment they would swap
partners and he would have Jessica in his arms
at last.

'It's good to see you happy.' Luca smiled, holding Jess lightly and allowing her to determine

the personal space she was comfortable with. 'Gio's a nice guy.'

'We're just friends,' Jess said for the umpteenth time.

Her protest produced a teasing chuckle. 'Right!'

'We *are*.' Jess sucked in a ragged breath and tried not to keep staring at Gio. Worst of all, she struggled to banish the ridiculous jealousy that swept through her as he danced with Polly. 'I can't get involved with anyone, Luca, you know that.'

Luca's expression sobered and he steered them to a quiet corner where they wouldn't be over-heard. 'I know nothing of the sort. You can have a normal relationship, Jess. I gather Gio doesn't know?'

'No.' A shiver rippled through her. 'He'd run a mile—like everyone else—if he did.' She hated the bitterness in her voice but the lessons of the last four years had been learned the hard way. 'Gio's still grieving. Even were he not, no man would want someone like me.'

'You're wrong, Jess. And you're doing Gio a big

disservice,' he cautioned, his words forestalling a further protest from her. 'Give him a chance. He cares about you and knows what a wonderful woman you are. If he reacts as you fear, then he isn't worthy of you. But what if he understands? Think of all you then have to gain.'

Jess bit her lip, caught in an agony of indecision. She didn't want to lose what she already had and she didn't dare to believe she could have more.

'Don't condemn yourself to a lifetime alone. I nearly did. I was so fearful of being hurt again, but my life is so enriched thanks to Polly. Think about it,' he added, guiding her back onto the dance floor. 'It might sound like a cliché, but none of us knows what the future holds so live each day to the fullest and allow yourself to love and be loved.'

It sounded simple when Luca put it into words, but Jess knew it was anything *but* simple in reality. So distracted was she that she didn't notice Luca steering her towards Gio and Polly, but in the next moment she found herself in Gio's arms as Luca reclaimed his wife. Oh, hell! She hadn't intended dancing at all, and certainly not with Gio because of the temptation when she was near him. But she couldn't make a scene in front of everyone.

She held herself stiffly as he drew her closer, his touch, his scent, the feel of his body brushing against hers having a potent affect on her. One dance wouldn't hurt, would it? One moment out of time to enjoy being in his arms, forgetting why she had to be strong?

As she relaxed, giving up the fight, Gio drew her closer, making her even more aware of him, her body instinctively responding to his nearness. When the music ended, she sighed and made a half-hearted effort to draw away.

'Stay. Please.' The throaty warmth of his voice stripped her of any remaining willpower and common sense.

The tempo slowed and Jess found herself pressed far too intimately against him, her arms winding round him of their own volition. His fingertips brushed the bare skin between her shoulder blades, exposed by the V back of the dress, making her burn with a rush of desire. She was oblivious to everyone else, focused only on Gio, every sense heightened and attuned to him.

He bent his head, the warmth of his breath caressing her neck, the brush of his faintly stubbled jaw against her sensitive skin incredibly erotic. She'd never expected to be held again, let alone dance in public. Emotion threatened to overwhelm her and, to her horror, tears stung her eyes. She buried her face against his chest to hide them…from him and anyone else.

Revelling in this opportunity to hold Jessica properly for the first time, Gio breathed in her unique womanly scent mixed with the familiar hint of chocolate that clung to her hair and skin. Hair and skin that felt super-soft beneath his fingertips.

He was conscious of her heightened emotions, although he doubted she was aware of the way she was clinging to him. Determined not to rush or scare her, he held her, swaying to the music and waiting for her to relax, welcoming the moment she gave up whatever inner battle she was fighting and melted into him. She felt so right in his arms, her curvy body a perfect fit for his.

'Ready to go home?' he asked some considerable time later as they stepped outside to get some fresh air. He wanted her to himself, relishing these moments when he felt closer to her than ever.

She tipped her head back and looked up at the night sky. 'Yes, please.'

After saying goodbye and gathering up their belongings, they drove home in good spirits and were greeted by two sleepy kittens, who stirred long enough to be cuddled. As Jessica settled them again, he went through to the kitchen.

'Hot chocolate?' he asked, smiling at the look on her face.

'Lovely!'

'I'll make it for you the proper Italian way. None of this powdered cocoa with water in a microwave.' He gave an exaggerated shudder of disgust, making her laugh.

'And what is the proper Italian way?'

He took a large bar of *Cioccolato Corezzi's* finest dark chocolate from his stash in a kitchen drawer. 'You must begin with real chocolate. Once melted, you add a little sugar and some milk, bring it to the boil and stir. Some people make it so thick it is like a mousse and has to be eaten with a spoon,' he explained as he broke squares of chocolate and dropped them into a bowl, the satisfying snap a sign of its high quality. 'I prefer it liquid enough to drink, although I keep the teaspoon to reach the last drops!'

'It sounds sinfully delicious.'

It was Jessica who was sinfully delicious. Looking at her fired his blood and stirred his body. Waiting for the water to heat, he leaned his hip against the worktop and watched as she sat at the counter, trying to undo the barrette clasp that held her ponytail in place. Something was stuck and as she muttered to herself, making him smile, he stepped in to help.

'May I?'

Before she had the chance to refuse, he moved behind her, feeling her tense as his fingers set to work. Within moments the clip was free. Unable to resist temptation, his fingers burrowed into the fiery mass of curls that tumbled around her shoulders.

'You have beautiful hair,' he told her, hearing the roughness in his voice.

She gave a shaky laugh. 'I used to hate it.'

'No! It's amazing. Silky soft.' He leaned closer and caught the scent of her chocolatey shampoo. 'And you smell so good.'

'Gio...' Her voice sounded husky and sensual.

The sexual tension increased, electricity crackling between them. Jessica slowly slid round on the stool until she was facing him, olive-green eyes dark with awareness and unmistakeable desire.

His breath caught. 'I *have* to kiss you,' he whispered roughly.

A tremor ran through her but she didn't move away. His hands fisted in her hair as he closed the gap millimetre by millimetre, his heart thudding a rapid tattoo. Finally, their lips met. He felt heady with excitement and yet incredibly nervous as he kissed her for the first time.

They were both tentative, finding their way,

learning, savouring, exploring, but the passion quickly flared out of control. Jessica's lips parted and he tilted his head, deepening the kiss. She tasted like heaven. Sweet and sensual, and so addictive. He couldn't get his fill of her. Tongues met, stroked, tempted, and he heard her soft, needy whimper as she clung to him. One hand left her hair and he wrapped his arm around her waist, drawing her into him as he stepped up between her parted thighs. She wriggled closer, pressing herself against him.

Jessica was with him, taking and giving, meeting and matching the blaze of passion that flared so intensely between them, demanding more. Gio was all too aware when instant panic set in and she began to withdraw. With a sharp cry she pulled away from him, clearly distressed.

'What is it, *fiamma?*' he asked between ragged breaths, confused and concerned as tears spilled from eyes full of torment. 'What's wrong?'

She shook her head. 'I'm sorry. So sorry. I can't do this.'

Before he could respond, she pushed away from him, slipped awkwardly off the stool and ran. He heard her footsteps on the stairs and, moments later, the sound of her bedroom door closing. What the hell had happened? Running an unsteady hand through his hair, he took a moment to gather himself together and get his body, so unused to the fiery passion that had ignited between them, back under control.

No way could he leave Jessica in such a distressed state. He wanted to know what had gone wrong, but more important was his concern for her well-being. After checking the house was secure and the kittens were settled, he finished making the hot chocolate and carried two mugs upstairs, anxious about what he might find. Taking a deep breath, he knocked on the door.

'Jessica?'

There was silence for several moments, a silence that hung so heavily around him that he could hear each beat of his heart. 'Yes?' The word was so soft that had he not been listening so intently he would not have heard her.

Cautiously, he opened the door. Dressed now in unflattering but comfortable pyjamas, Jessica was sitting in the middle of the bed, her arms wrapped around herself as she rocked slightly to and fro. She looked so lost, vulnerable and scared that his heart, which he'd thought could never feel anything again, squeezed with pain for her…and such deep affection and longing he didn't dare examine the emotions too deeply.

'May I come in?' His heart was in his mouth as he waited for her decision.

She didn't meet his gaze, but finally she nodded. He sat on the edge of the bed, careful not to crowd her. He handed her a mug, noting that her hands were shaking as she reached for it, but she cupped it in her palms and sipped, a soft sigh escaping as she savoured the thick, chocolaty treat.

Gio followed her lead, hoping she would begin to relax. She even managed the ghost of a smile when he handed her a teaspoon so she could copy him and capture the final bits of chocolate.

'Good?' he asked, nearly having heart failure as her tongue peeped out and she licked the remains of chocolate from her lips.

'Amazing.' Her voice was still soft but sounded

stronger. Popping the spoon in the empty mug, she handed it to him. 'Thank you.'

Gio set the mugs aside, feeling a growing tension now the moment had come to seek answers to some questions.

'Jessica, we need to talk.' Once more she wrapped her arms around herself, lashes lowering to hide her expression, but not before he had seen the fear in her eyes. 'I need to know. I know you guard your personal space and avoid being touched. At first I thought it was me, then I noticed it was the same with everyone. Including your clever ruse using all that stuff you carry round the hospital so you can avoid shaking hands.'

The blush that brought colour back to her too-pale cheeks was confirmation that he was right.

'My imagination is running away with itself. I'm scared to ask but...has someone hurt you in the past?' He could hardly get the words out but knew he had to. 'Were you raped or abused?'

'No.'

The denial was firm and he knew she was

telling the truth. The relief was *huge*. But there was still something major and important. He knew it. She looked so alone, and the despair and hurt in her eyes tore him apart.

'May I hold you, Jessica…please?'

She raised her head and met his gaze. What she was searching for, he had no idea, but whatever it was, she apparently found it as, after the longest time, she bit her lip and nodded. The air trapped in his lungs was released in a rush of relief. He moved onto his knees and edged towards her, needing the physical contact as much as she did. When he was as close as could be, he sat back on his heels and drew her into his arms with infinite care, cradling her tense and shaking form against him.

As she gradually began to relax, she rested her head against his chest. With one hand he stroked the unrestrained glossy copper-red curls as they tumbled with abandon around her shoulders.

'Can you talk to me now?' A breath shuddered out of her in response. Her casual shrug belied the tension that poured from her and the tremble he felt ripple through her whole body. 'Jessica?'

'I don't know. I...'

The whispered words were husky with emotion and he sought to discover the cause of her hesitation and reluctance. 'What worries you, *fiamma*? Do you think I won't understand? Do you fear it will change how I think of you and feel about you?'

'I know it will,' she responded, the humourless laugh and bitter edge to her voice speaking volumes.

'Listen to me,' he instructed gently, seeking the words to reassure her. 'I don't know what experiences you've had with other people, but *nothing* you tell me will make me turn away or reject you.' Whatever route their relationship eventually took, he was unable to envisage any circumstance that would change the basic friendship and bond that had formed so quickly but so intensely between them. He dropped a kiss on the top of her head. 'Trust me. I won't let you down.'

* * *

The sincerity in Gio's voice was beyond question but Jess still hesitated. He might believe *now* that nothing would make him reject her but would he feel the same when he knew?

She recalled Luca's words. He'd advised her to give Gio a chance, pointing out that only by confiding in him would she discover the depth of his friendship and the kind of man he really was. Deep in her heart she knew. And she *so* wanted to believe. But her former friends and colleagues had turned her away and her family had disowned her.

The last few weeks with Gio had been the happiest she had known for such a long time and she was terrified that revealing the truth about herself would change for ever the nature of their friendship, maybe even end it. She didn't want to lose what she already had, but every day things were becoming more complicated because her heart and emotions were ever more entangled and it was no longer enough just to be his friend.

Those moments in the kitchen when she had allowed herself to wallow in the pleasure of being touched, followed by the most explosive and incredible kiss she had ever known, had proved that. He had breached her defences so completely and she'd been so lost in Gio and her desire for him that she'd forgotten why she shouldn't have been doing it. Reality had hit like a thunderclap and she'd run. They'd crossed the boundaries of friendship now. And in reaching for more, would she destroy what she already had?

She wouldn't know the answer unless she did as Gio asked and trusted him. Cocooned in his embrace she felt safe and protected and, for the first time in over four years, she didn't feel alone. She sucked in a deep breath, inhaling the warm musky-male scent of him that had become so familiar. And arousing. Drawing back just far enough, she looked up and met his steady, intensely blue gaze. While the arm supporting her cuddled her close, his free hand caught one of hers, raising it to his mouth and pressing a kiss to her palm before he entwined their fingers, linking them and giving her his support.

'I don't know where to start,' she admitted with a nervous laugh, feeling sick inside now the decision was made and the moment had come to share her shameful secret.

'Take your time. I'm not going anywhere,' he promised. 'Is it something that goes back to the time before you came to St Piran?'

'Yes. It started just over four years ago when I was still in Scotland,' she admitted, closing her eyes as the memories flooded back. She paused, unsure if she could continue, but Gio's support and strength gave her the courage to face what had to be faced. 'I was working in a hospital there,' she explained, ignoring for now the information about her former career. 'I was living with my fiancé, Duncan. He was my first and only proper boyfriend. I was happy. I thought I had everything I wanted, and I was busy planning the wedding, which was only eight weeks away.'

As Jessica gathered her thoughts, Gio struggled with the unreasonable jealousy that assailed him at the knowledge she had been in love and about to be married, already disliking the man she spoke of without knowing any more about him.

But he hid his reaction, needing to give her all his understanding now that she had done him the honour of trusting him. He couldn't—wouldn't—let her down.

'Did Duncan work at the hospital, too?' he asked, keeping his tone neutral.

'No. He worked for a company that supplied equipment and aid for relief charities out in the field and his job took him all over the world. He was away a lot. I missed him, but I supported what he did.'

He was unsurprised by her selflessness and the sacrifices she'd no doubt made. 'It's not easy maintaining a relationship long distance.'

'No.' Another shiver ran through her and he tightened his hold, wanting to protect her from the hurt she was reliving. 'I hadn't been feeling well for a while,' she continued, and his concern for her increased. 'There was nothing specific I could put my finger on, and I put it down to the pressures of work and the excitement and lack of sleep as the wedding drew closer. Duncan had to take several trips away during those weeks and so everything fell to me. A colleague noticed how off colour I was and suggested I see a doctor. I didn't think anything of it, but because I wanted to feel right for the wedding, I made an appointment to see my GP.'

Gio felt his gut tightening with the premonition that something dark and of huge importance was about to be revealed. Looking into green eyes shadowed with fear and pain, it was the dart of shame that confused him. He raised their joined hands, pressing a kiss to her fingers.

'What happened, *fiamma*?' he prompted.

'My GP didn't think there was anything serious going on, but he organised some tests to be on the safe side. And…' She halted, her voice breaking, tears shimmering on long sooty lashes.

Gio steeled himself for whatever was to come. 'And?'

'The results came back.' A sob tore through her, ripping him to shreds. 'It t-turned out that D-Duncan hadn't been the f-faithful, loving fiancé I'd imagined,' she continued, the words stuttering through her tears. 'He'd slept with countless women during his trips abroad and thanks to him I h-have a lasting legacy. The tests, unlike Duncan, didn't lie. I...' Again she broke off, drawing in a shuddering breath, her fingers instinctively tightening on his as she raised her head, tear-washed eyes bleak. 'Gio, I was...*am*... HIV positive.'

CHAPTER NINE

'Madre del Dio.'

The words escaped on a whisper of breath when all Gio wanted to do was rage and swear at the man who had done this to Jessica. He listened as she told him how she had been diagnosed with a seroconversion illness and although it was not his branch of medicine, he knew enough to understand that this was often the first sign of illness people had after they had been infected, when the body first produced antibodies to HIV.

'I had many of the usual symptoms…a fever, aching limbs, headache and a blotchy red rash… which could have been linked to a variety of conditions,' she explained, the matter-of-fact tone of her voice belied by the shadows in her eyes. 'It was such a shock and not something I had ever anticipated.'

'Of course not. You trusted the man you were about to marry,' Gio reasoned.

She nodded, and he tightened his hold as a fresh shudder went through her. 'I must be a really bad person because I can't forgive him— not just for what he did to me but I keep thinking about the unknown number of other women out there he infected, as well, and what they might be going through. I can't even feel sorry that he was diagnosed, too,' she whispered.

'No, no, no! You are not remotely a bad person! How can you think that?' Gio swore in Italian, wishing he could let Duncan know what he thought of him. 'You are an amazing woman, Jessica. Even struggling to come to terms with what has happened to you, through no fault of your own, your thoughts are still for other people. You have the generosity of spirit to worry about the women with whom your ex-fiancé—' he stumbled over the word, choked by his anger and disgust at the man '—had been unfaithful.'

'It wasn't their fault. I've no doubt he lied to them, too.'

'And now,' he made himself ask, needing to

know so much but anxious not to stress her more, 'how are you? Are you taking medication?'

'I'm OK. And I'm not taking medication yet,' she told him, and the relief was immense. 'I have regular tests to monitor my CD4 cell count, which gives an idea of the strength of my immune system. And a viral load test, which can tell how active HIV is in the body. It's only if those levels reach a certain point that medication will be necessary. It's a big step to take because once started, you can't stop. I go to London twice a year to see a specialist,' she added, surprising him.

'Why London?'

'I went there first when I left Scotland. I trust Mr Jackson. When I moved to Cornwall, he agreed to keep seeing me.' Her smile was tired but brought some life back to her eyes. 'And I have Luca and the other doctors at the Penhally surgery who take care of day-to-day things.'

Gio was relieved she had someone so good caring for her. 'Was there no one giving you support at home? What about family and friends?'

he asked, taken aback by her derisive, humour-less laugh. Unease curled inside him.

'I was stupidly naïve and assumed that in this day and age people would be more informed and understanding,' she began with a shiver, shifting so that she was resting against his chest. 'But they weren't. I was so shocked by the negative reactions. Some people blanked me, some were openly hostile and abusive, making a big fuss if I touched them in any way, refusing to drink from a mug or eat off a plate I might have used in the canteen. Not one so-called friend or colleague stood by me.'

As he listened to Jessica outline some of the things people had said to her and what she had put up with once her diagnosis had become known, Gio's anger rocketed. It was disgraceful that people should be so ignorant and prejudiced. And it was hardly surprising after her experiences that she'd been stripped of her confidence, her self-esteem and her trust in people.

'My family were worse.'

'What happened, *fiamma*?' he asked softly, fearing her answer.

'Shocked and upset, I went home and told them the news. My father has always been a dour, strict man with rigid opinions. He disapproved of me living with Duncan before the wedding. He said…' Her fingers tightened on his and emotion turned her voice husky as she continued. 'He said it was all I deserved for living in sin, that I had brought shame on the family, and he disowned me. He turned me out with all my belongings and told me never to contact them again. He even had me barred from visiting my grandmother, who was bedridden in a nursing home by then. She was the only one who cared. She left me the money that helped me buy my cottage, but I never had the chance to see her again before she died and tell her I loved her.'

Her words ended on a sob and the tears she had been choking back escaped. She tried to pull away from him but he drew her trembling frame more fully against him and, wrapping her protectively in his arms, he held her tight, keeping her safe as she cried out the hurt and anger. After everything Duncan had done, and the reaction of those she'd considered friends, the cruel rejection by the family meant to love and care for her must have been the ultimate betrayal and almost impossible to bear. Thinking of her alone and scared tore him apart.

He guessed she'd been bottling up the emotion for a long time and now it had been set free, like opening a dam and allowing everything backed up behind it to gush out. As he cradled her, he struggled to come to terms with the truth, the reality, the consequences…and with what her life must have been like these last four or more years.

His own eyes were moist and his heart hurt as he tried to comfort her while the storm ran its course. So many things now made sense. Her reluctance to touch and be touched, the absence of any close friendships, the lack of trust and the little habits at home like the supplements and washing her things separately. No wonder she had looked so hurt when he'd teased her about having a hygiene fetish. He smothered a groan. After all she had been through since being diagnosed, it was understandable she had developed a range of coping mechanisms.

When Jessica finally calmed, he eased back and cupped her face in his hands. Olive-green eyes were framed by tear-spiked lashes while her flawless, translucent skin was devoid of colour. Concerned for her, he dropped a light kiss on lips that still trembled.

'Don't go anywhere. I'll be back in a couple of minutes. OK?'

Her nod was weary, almost defeated. Reluctantly, he released her. He didn't want to leave her, even for a moment, but he had a few things to do. When he returned, having undressed as far as his boxer shorts, prepared his bedroom with jasmine-scented candles and turned down the bed, she was sitting motionless where he had left her, her eyes closed.

'Jessica?'

Long lashes flickered then he was staring into her eyes. She blinked, her gaze skimming over him, a flush bringing some warmth back to her pale face. Her reaction amused him, momentarily easing his concern for her.

'Hi.' He smiled as she swallowed and dragged her gaze back to his. 'Are you OK?'

She nodded, remaining silent until his next moved shocked her out of her torpor. 'Gio!' Her cry escaped as he scooped her off the bed and lifted her in his arms.

'Hold on,' he instructed.

'What are you doing?' Despite her protest, she wrapped her arms around his neck. 'Gio, I'm far too heavy.'

'Nonsense.'

He carried her from the room, only pausing long enough for her to switch out the light. Walking down the corridor, he went into his bedroom, set her gently on the bed and drew the duvet over her before walking round the other side and sliding in beside her. To his surprise and delight, she turned into his arms and burrowed into him. He stroked the glossy curls that spread across his chest, each indrawn breath fragranced with a teasing hint of her scent.

'Gio…' Her voice was soft and sleepy, and it still held the lingering legacy of the emotions that had ravaged her just a short while ago.

'Shh,' he soothed, relishing the feel of her feminine curves and the softness of her skin.

'It's very late and you've been through a lot. Sleep now. I'll keep you safe.'

It was Sunday afternoon and the closer they got to home, the more nervous Jess became. She knew what was going to happen. She wanted it. And yet she couldn't help but be as scared as she was excited. Gio, too, seemed preoccupied and edgy as the electric tension continued to build between them.

She thought back to the night before and everything that had happened after their return from the wedding and the most incredible kiss she'd ever experienced. Telling Gio how her life had been turned upside down following the HIV diagnosis had been so difficult, but he had been amazing, his supportive reaction in marked contrast to those she had encountered in the past. But now her shameful secret was out, nothing would ever be the same between them again.

Spending the night in Gio's arms had been wonderful. For the first time in a long, long while she hadn't felt alone. And she wished she could wake up with him every morning, especially if it meant experiencing the delicious caress of his hands and his lips on her bare skin.

'I want more than anything to make love to you,' he'd told her, the throaty roughness of his voice resonating along her nerve-endings. 'I have since the day I first saw you, and I've wanted you more each day since.'

'Gio,' she'd murmured in confusion, hardly daring to believe that the truth hadn't put him off. He may have held her through the night, but…

'Nothing you have told me changes anything— I only marvel more at what an incredible woman you are,' he'd continued, his words bringing a lump to her throat. 'Unfortunately, right now I have no protection.'

She had masked her disappointment. 'OK.'

'But we can improvise.' The tone of his voice and his sexy smile had sent a tremor right through her. 'We can't make love fully now but I want to bring you pleasure and show what a special and desirable woman you are.'

And bring her pleasure he had. Oh, my! A shaky little breath escaped, warmth stealing through her as her body tingled at the memory of his kisses and caresses. How delicious to wake up like that every day. But she knew it was a fantasy. She was getting too far ahead of herself.

They'd spent the day doing normal things at the house, having a late breakfast and playing with the kittens before going to see how things were progressing at her cottage. The main supporting structure had been replaced and the thatcher was well on the way to creating a beautiful new roof.

Knowing that the cottage would soon be habitable again and discovering that Gio had arranged for the fields to be cleared and the fences renewed in readiness for Faye's menagerie had brought mixed emotions. Pleasure at seeing the cottage come back to life. Surprise and gratitude at Gio's generosity. But anxiety at the knowledge she would soon have to leave his house—and him. What would happen then? Gio was adamant about sharing responsibility for the animals but how would that work? And what did it mean for them?

Next, they'd spent a couple of hours on the

boat, speeding across the waves. She'd felt so close to him and, now her secret was out, she hadn't had to fight to avoid physical contact. Gio had taken every opportunity to hug and kiss her. But her nervousness had returned when they had stopped at the supermarket on the way back to the house and condoms had been added to the items in their basket.

Feeling jumpy and on edge, not at all sure what to do or say, Jess helped Gio put the shopping away and then played with Dickens and Kipling for a while before feeding them. As they curled up to sleep in a tangle of limbs, she felt even more anxious.

'I think I'll go and have a shower,' she murmured, feeling as gauche and awkward as a teenager.

Gio looked up and smiled. 'OK.'

He appeared so calm that had he not bought the condoms she would have wondered if she had dreamed everything that had happened when she had woken up that morning. And what she was anticipating would happen later. Unsettled, she went upstairs and, after undressing and tying up her wayward curls to keep her hair from getting wet, she stepped into the shower, welcoming the feel of the hot barbs on skin that still felt alive and sensitive from the caresses of Gio's hands and mouth.

Eyes closed, she tipped her head back and reached out a hand for the chocolate-scented cleanser she loved to use, a squeal of shocked surprise escaping as, instead of encountering the plastic tube she was expecting, her fingers met male skin. Every part of her trembled as he stepped up behind her, the front of his body pressing against the back of hers, making her supremely aware of his arousal.

She heard the snap of the top on the tube she'd been reaching for and a moment later felt the touch of hands that were slick with foamy cleanser. He began at her shoulders, working slowly and sensually down her back, lingering at her rear before sweeping down her legs in long, caressing strokes that turned her knees to jelly. One arm wrapped around her waist in support, and she leaned back against him, feeling boneless and on fire as he turned his attention to the front of her.

Jess bit her lip to prevent herself crying out as he devoted time to her breasts, the exquisite torture almost too much to bear. It had been so long since she had been touched like this…and yet *never* like this because the kind of explosive passion and intense desire she shared with Gio was way beyond anything she had ever experienced before.

When she thought she would expire from the pleasure of his touch, Gio turned the cleanser over to her and allowed her the same freedom to explore and enjoy his body. She turned round on legs that felt decidedly unsteady, the blood racing through her veins as she drank in the sight of him. It was impossible not to be struck by the masculine beauty of his body, the broad shoulders and the perfectly toned muscles of his arms and torso that made her mouth water. A brush of dark hair in the middle of his chest cast a shadow on olive-toned skin, tapering to a narrow line that her gaze avidly followed down over his abdomen and navel to where it nested the potent symbol of his maleness.

She refocused on his handsome face, seeing the needy desire, which mirrored her own, in his deeply blue eyes. Feeling both shy and bold at the same time, she began her own lingering caress of his body, working the foamy, chocolate-scented suds across his skin, hearing his indrawn breath and feeling the tremor and ripple of muscle as he reacted to her touch.

With an impatient exclamation his hands closed on her upper arms, drawing her back up and into a searing kiss. She clung to him, kissing him back with equal ardour, savouring the feel of wet warm skin under her hands and the sexy, sinful taste of him in her mouth. They were both breathing heavily by the time they broke apart. Gio snapped off the water before reaching for a towel and wrapping her up in it. With evident impatience he briskly ran another towel over himself. Tossing it aside, he took her hand and led her down the corridor to his bedroom, her legs so rubbery she didn't think she could walk.

Some of her anxiety returned as she entered the room with him and saw the huge bed standing ready and waiting, the duvet turned back, the generous pillows plumped up. She knew how luxurious and incredibly sexy the gunmetal-grey sheets felt against her skin. And within moments she was experiencing them again as Gio gave her a gentle rub down with the towel before removing it and tumbling them both into bed.

Excitement and tension vied for prominence. She could feel the heat of his body even though he wasn't quite touching her. Smiling, he gently removed the pins from her hair and fanned the tresses out on the pillow.

'Do you think you are the only one who is nervous, *fiamma*?' he asked, his throaty, accented voice sounding even more sexy than usual.

Surprised, she met his gaze. 'You're nervous, too?'

Her question was met with a wry laugh. 'I listen to some of the young doctors talking in the scrub room and the canteen, discussing their conquests, and I realise what an oddity I must seem for having slept only with Sofia.'

'Then I'm odd, too, because I've only ever had one relationship before,' she told him. 'And, to me, the fact that you have never been the kind of man to sleep around is a major strength, not a weakness. You are loyal and true. And you haven't played Russian roulette with your own health or anyone else's.'

She thought of Duncan, of how he had cheated on her, and his cavalier disregard for himself, let alone her or the other women. Gio was a treasure and it was the very quality he considered an oddity that made her trust him. Had he been another Duncan, she would never be here now, on the cusp of giving herself to him in the most elemental of ways.

As if by instinct, they moved in unison to close the last of the gap between them, and the instant he touched her, the instant her lips met his, the doubts that had seemed so real for a moment dissolved into nothing. They needed no words because their bodies talked for them. Jess found she couldn't formulate a single coherent thought as Gio continued what he had begun that morning and in the shower, devoting his time and attention to her.

Every touch, every kiss, every caress of his fingers and brush of his lips and tongue built the pleasure layer by layer. She writhed against him, her body turning molten as his mouth worked down the column of her throat, setting every nerve tingling and every particle of skin on fire. He trailed down the valley between her breasts, bypassing flesh that yearned so badly for his attention and continuing down to her navel. She hadn't known she was so sensitive there but the tantalising, teasing quest of his teeth and tongue had her body arching up to meet him, seeking more.

She must have spoken the word aloud because he chuckled, the huff of warm breath against her skin a subtle and teasing caress of its own. She moaned as he finally turned his attention to her breasts, the perfect pressure of his fingers driving her crazy.

'Gio, please,' she begged, craving the touches he teasingly denied her.

Relenting, his teeth gently grazed one sensitive

nipple before his tongue salved the delicious sting. Then he sent her to the stratosphere as he took the peak into the warm cavern of his mouth. When she thought she couldn't bear it a moment longer he released his prize, turned his attention to its twin and began the exquisite torment all over again.

Impatient, her eager hands traced the muscular contours of his shoulders before working down his back, urging him closer. She wanted to explore and savour him as he was doing to her, but she was so close to the edge she couldn't wait a moment longer to know the joy of being united fully with him.

He took a moment to protect them and she pleaded with him not to wait any longer as he moved to make them one. She arched up to meet him, wrapping her legs around him, gasping his name at the delicious sensations as her body welcomed his and, finally, they were one.

'Jessica…'

'Yes. Please, Gio. Don't stop.'

She had never experienced anything as magical and special as making love with Gio. It was incredible, earth-shattering and she never wanted it to end. He murmured to her in Italian as they moved together in a rhythm as old as time. She abandoned herself to him completely, as he did to her, and the mix of exquisite tenderness and fiery passion she found with him was a devastating combination.

When the inevitable moment arrived, Jess clung to him, burying her face against him, breathing in his musky scent, calling his name as they drove each other over the edge to a shattering release. As she spun out of control, she didn't care if she never came down to earth again, just so long as she was with Gio.

Gio gazed at Jessica's sleeping form, the wild fire of her hair tossed across the pillow and a couple of tell-tale little marks on her otherwise flawless, silky-smooth skin following the intensely passionate night they had shared. It had been the most incredible experience, beyond anything he had imagined. And it had scared him.

He wasn't sure at exactly which moment during

their sensual night together it had happened, but he had suddenly known with surety and not much surprise that he loved her. It may have happened far more speedily but, as with Sofia, they had begun as friends first and foremost. He and Sofia had been children and their emotions had evolved slowly, whereas with Jessica the friendship and the desire had hit in tandem.

The pain of losing Sofia had nearly killed him and he'd never imagined wanting another woman again. Then he had met Jessica. He not only wanted her in every way but he liked and respected her as a person and valued the special friendship they shared. So why was he feeling so unsettled? Things had happened so fast, he had fallen so deep so quickly and he knew that if he tied himself to her and anything happened, he would never recover a second time.

Could he take the risk on Jessica's health? All he knew was that he couldn't face the prospect of burying another woman he loved. It was a possibility he couldn't ignore when making a decision that would affect both their futures.

* * *

Waking up alone had been unnerving and when she went downstairs and found Gio making coffee in the kitchen, Jess's unease increased. He greeted her with a smile, but she sensed a change in him. He was on edge, distant. And when he backed off physically, moving away when she would have stepped in for a hug, a cold chill went through her.

'What's wrong?' she asked, fear building as he failed to meet her gaze.

'Nothing. I...'

'Gio?'

He ran a hand through his hair, a characteristic sign of agitation. 'I'm just not sure what to think about this. It's all happened so quickly.'

'You regret it.' Her heart sank.

'No! Of course not. Neither of us was expecting this. The connection was there from the first and our friendship is special and important to me,' he explained, his expression sombre, and Jess sensed a 'but' coming. 'But—' Jess allowed herself a humourless smile '—maybe we should slow things down, take some time. I'd never considered having a new relationship. I'm not sure

I'm ready. Especially after what happened with Sofia.'

Everything in her screamed in protest. 'I see.'

'I need to be sure, Jessica. Not of you but of me. Losing Sofia nearly killed me and I can't go through anything like that again,' he finished, emotion heavy in his voice.

The awful thing was that she understood. She couldn't argue against his words and the chance of something happening was greater with her with the HIV hanging over her head than it was with another woman. Wrapping her arms around herself, she tried to hold everything together, to not let him see how deeply the rejection had wounded her. Because that was what it felt like. And in that moment, the truth hit home with devastating force…she loved him. In every way and with every part of her being.

Gio had said their friendship was important and apparently he considered things would go on as before, but Jess felt as if part of her was dying inside because friendship was never going to be enough now.

'I'm going to Italy at the weekend for my parents' fortieth wedding anniversary,' he reminded her, thrusting his hands into the pockets of his jeans.

Her heart breaking, Jess struggled to keep her voice as normal as possible. 'My cottage should be ready by then, so I'll move out.'

'I didn't mean that.' He frowned as if her leaving was not something he had considered.

'Living here was only meant to be temporary,' she pointed out, knowing she couldn't stay with him and not *be with* him. 'It's for the best.'

His frown deepened, confusion and disappointment mingling in his intensely blue eyes. 'If that's what you want.'

It wasn't what she wanted at all, but she didn't see how she could do anything else if what she really wanted—Gio himself—was not an option.

The next few days were like purgatory, and by the time Friday arrived, Jess was at breaking point and not at all sure how much longer she could hold on. Pretending to accept Gio's decision to return things to a platonic footing had involved the performance of her life. She hadn't been able to sleep, lying in a bed a short distance down the corridor from him, wanting more than anything to be in his arms. But it wasn't going to happen and the sooner she faced that and rebuilt her battered defences, the better it would be.

He went to Italy on the Friday and, after the loneliest night in the house without him, Jess tried to hold back the tears as she packed her things into her car and then put Dickens and Kipling into their basket for the short journey to her cottage. The kittens would miss Gio almost as much as she would, she reflected sadly. He'd been so good with them. She choked back the emotion as she recalled the way he had lain on the floor, chuckling as the two growing kittens had romped over him. And the time she'd come in late one Friday night after her session of volunteering at the Samaritans to find Gio lying asleep on the sofa, the kittens curled up on his chest in a tangle.

Feeling numb inside, she secured the house and drove away from it, wondering if it was for the last time. However much she hurt, she couldn't blame Gio. She knew how devastating Sofia's death had been and it was understandable that he was wary of embarking on another relationship, especially with someone like her. She was well at the moment, and she would do all she could to stay that way. As Luca and her specialist, Mr Jackson, frequently told her, there was no reason why she couldn't live into old age with very few problems at all. But anyone would be wary of taking on that uncertainty, especially someone who had experienced what Gio had.

No, Gio was not to blame. It was her own fault. She'd hoped for too much…had dared to dream and to believe in the impossible. Now she had to pick up the pieces because fairy-tale, happy-ever-after endings didn't happen to people like her.

'Why did you stay the night with me?'
It was one of the things Megan had most dreaded Josh ever asking and it had played over and over in her head since the day in A and E

when they had done the unthinkable and faced their past.

Aside from not wanting to acknowledge the truth to herself, she certainly didn't want to tell *Josh* the answer to his question. To admit that she had been drawn to him from the first moment she had seen him and that, despite his reputation, she had yearned for him for years like some lovestruck teenager was beyond embarrassing.

Between medical school and caring for her grandmother, she'd had no time for a social life, so going to a party on New Year's Eve had been a real treat. Wearing an exquisite dress, her hair and make-up done, she'd felt like Cinderella. Only she'd been granted a bit longer before the spell had been broken…not at midnight, for her, but lunchtime the following day.

For the first time, Josh had approached her. Given his undivided attention, she'd melted like an ice cube under the noon sun. He'd made her feel special. Surprisingly, they had talked and talked, and she'd found him so much *more* than she had ever expected. He'd been funny, he'd listened as if what she'd had to say had mattered, he'd sympathised about her grandmother, and he had confided in her, too. The night had ended in the inevitable way, the sexual chemistry and tension between them impossible to resist.

Megan closed her eyes and tried to push away the painful memories. She had believed in her heart that what they had shared had been more than one night. Much more. Or she never would have gone home with Josh in the first place. They'd connected. On every level. She hadn't imagined it. And it *hadn't* just been the sex, amazing as that had been. She knew Josh had been spooked by their closeness as he'd freely admitted that he'd revealed things to her that he'd never told to anyone else. He'd told her she was different. He'd been so genuine. And she'd believed him. Had *wanted* to believe him. So badly.

They had finally, reluctantly, parted but only after Josh had made love to her one last time and had made her promise to meet him that evening. It had been noon when she had rushed home to her grandmother feeling a mix of guilt and euphoria. The hours with Josh had been the most amazing of her life and she hadn't been able to wait to see him again. So when he had stood her up, failing to meet at the agreed time and place, she had been confused and upset.

When she had finally seen him several worrying days later, he had blanked her completely, laughing with his friends, ignoring her as if their night had never happened. She'd been devastated. Even now she could remember how she had felt... used, cheap, stupid, incredibly naïve and very, very hurt.

Megan shivered in reaction as the memories of that lonely, frightening time and what had followed over the next months flowed through her. Ashamed, she had withdrawn and hidden herself away. And then she had discovered that she was pregnant. And *so* scared.

Weeks later she'd experienced a searing pain and had remembered nothing until she had woken up in hospital to learn that Josh had been part of the team who had not only taken away her baby but had performed a hysterectomy, depriving her of ever becoming a mother. She'd been devastated, the sense of loss and grief overwhelming.

Eight years on, listening to his explanation and seeing his own emotion had given her much to think about. The hurt remained, both at his rejection and at the loss of her baby. But while there was much she was still angry with him about, she no longer blamed him for the miscarriage or the lengths taken to save her life.

Despite their past and all that lay between them—including the very real presence of his wife—the chemistry remained. When they worked together in A and E, they often knew what the other was thinking or doing without the need for words.

She knew he was out of bounds. She knew what had happened the last time the chemistry had led her astray. And she couldn't forget the way Josh had rejected and betrayed her. So discovering that she was still vulnerable to him, still drawn to him and still unable to get him out of her mind, frightened her.

If she showed the slightest weakness she feared what might happen. And only heartache would lie ahead. She had learned her lesson the hard way the last time round. So why did she have the terrible feeling that history was going to repeat itself?

CHAPTER TEN

LATE on Sunday afternoon Jess walked along the surfing beach east of Penhally's harbour, lost in thought. It had been another beautiful day, but the air was cooling as the sun began its slow descent towards the horizon. Pushing her hands into the pockets of the floaty skirt that fell to her knees, Jess sighed. There was no escaping her thoughts. Thoughts that were stuck in one place and refused to budge. With Gio.

He would be back tonight and tomorrow she would see him at work. She wasn't sure how to continue pretending that nothing had happened or behave normally, accepting they could only ever be friends. *Could* she be friends when she wanted so much more? It was a question that had pounded in her head all week and she still didn't know the answer. All she did know was that she had missed him terribly and faced with a choice of never seeing him again, then, as sad and pathetic as it sounded, any part of Gio was better than no Gio at all. Even if she was dying inside. Because she had fallen in love with a man who had experienced such heartache that he couldn't take a risk on someone whose future could be as uncertain as hers.

As she neared the end of the promontory on which the lighthouse, coastguard office and St Mark's church stood, she heard shouting and laughter, and looked up to see a couple of teenagers messing about on the rocks. She was about to turn round and retrace her steps back along the beach when the tone of the teenage voices changed and she watched in horror as one of the boys lost his footing and crashed face down amongst the rocks.

Jess ran towards the scene of the accident, as did a few other people who were further away on the beach and up on the promontory. The teenager's friend was now silent and standing motionless in shock and terror as he gazed down at his stricken comrade. Reaching the rocky outcrop, and glad she was wearing trainers, Jess began to climb.

The lower rocks were slippery, and several times she lost her own footing, resulting in umpteen cuts and bruises, but she kept going as rapidly as she could, fearing what she would find when she reached the boy. Moving towards him, she misjudged a step and fell heavily. Pain seared through her foot, leg and side, and she felt the hot stickiness of blood flowing down her calf. Ignoring it, she limped and scrambled awkwardly the rest of the way to the boy.

His injuries were worse than she'd feared. Frightened eyes stared up at her, and she struggled to mask her shock so as not to distress him further. His face had borne the brunt of his fall and, along with a lot of bleeding and considerable soft-tissue damage, she could tell that his jaw, nose and one cheekbone were all broken.

Instinct took over as she did a quick assessment. There were no other apparent injuries but that hardly mattered because there was one serious, immediate and life-threatening problem…

the boy was finding it increasingly impossible to breathe.

'Has anyone called an ambulance?' she shouted to the small crowd that was gathering on the rocks above her.

'Yes,' someone called. 'ETA at least twelve minutes.'

Jess swore. They couldn't wait that long. 'I need a sharp knife—preferably a scalpel. And something like a small piece of tube, or a drinking straw. Anything narrow and hollow. He can't breathe and I have to help him,' she shouted up.

'The lighthouse and coastguard station both have full first-aid kits. I'll get one of those,' the man called down to her.

'Please hurry! There isn't much time.'

Hoping the man understood the urgency, and that the kit would contain the things she needed, Jess returned her attention to the boy and tried to talk soothingly to him as she continued her assessment. With all the blood, fragments of bone and the rapidly swelling tissues around his face, there was no way she could clear or maintain an airway. It was no surprise when he began to panic as he failed to draw oxygen into his lungs and started to lose consciousness.

It seemed an eternity before the man reappeared above her and began the dangerous climb down. His exclamation of shock when he saw the boy was understandable but Jess didn't have time to do anything but take the first-aid kit from him. She winced at the shaft of pain in her side as she dragged the heavy bag close, but she pushed her own discomfort aside and opened the kit, giving heartfelt thanks that it was an extensive and well-stocked one.

Gathering together the things she needed, she told her unknown companion what she was doing. 'I have to create an opening in his throat so he can breathe. We can't wait for the ambulance. What's your name?'

'Charlie.'

'I'm Jess. I...' She paused and sucked in a breath. 'I'm a doctor,' she told him, speaking aloud the words she had not used for four years. 'Have you got a mobile phone, Charlie?'

'Yes, right here.'

'Phone 999 and tell them we need the air ambulance, too,' she requested, knowing that if what she attempted was successful, the boy would need to get to hospital as fast as possible.

As Charlie made the call, Jess focused on the task ahead. Nervousness gripped her. Shutting out the comments from the small crowds on the rocks above her and the beach below, she steadied herself and called on all her former training. She was scared, but she'd done this a few times before. She could do it now. She had to if the boy wasn't to suffocate before the ambulance arrived. Closing her eyes, she did a quick mental run-through of the emergency procedure she had never expected to be called on to perform again.

After using an antiseptic wipe on the boy's throat, she draped some gauze around the site and then she took out the sterile, single-use blade that was in the kit. She had no local anaesthetic available, but with his consciousness level low he probably didn't need it. Unsure how aware he was, she told him what she needed to do, talking through it as much to steady herself as him.

With the fingers of one hand she felt for the correct spot on the throat and, with her other hand, made a small vertical incision through the skin. Identifying the cricothyroid membrane, she made a horizontal cut through it, careful to ensure that she didn't damage the cartilage. With no proper tracheal spreader available she had to improvise again, and she used the handle of a small knife she found in the kit, inserting it into the incision and turning it so that it created a small passage. Already there was a life-saving flow of air in and out as the boy's lungs inflated and reinflated.

'Could you cut me some strips of tape, Charlie?'

As he obliged, Jess cut a piece of plastic tube to the right length and, with great care so as not to damage any cartilage or the vocal cords, angled it and slid it into the makeshift passageway. It was a temporary measure but it would keep the boy alive and his airway open until the paramedics arrived. Taking the strips Charlie handed her, she secured the tube in place.

'Well done, Jess!' Charlie praised when she

had finished, giving a thumbs-up to the crowd on the promontory and beach, who broke into spontaneous applause.

Jess sat back and let out a shaky breath. 'Thanks.'

It had only taken two or three minutes to complete the procedure and yet she felt weary and quite unsteady. Taking the boy's hand, she continued to monitor his breathing, relieved that he was awake. She gently wiped away the blood from around his eyes—brown eyes that were now open again and staring at her with a mix of relief and fright and pain.

'The ambulance will be here very soon,' she reassured him, rewarded when his fingers tightened on hers.

He was going to need an excellent maxillofacial surgeon for reconstruction, Jess reflected, her thoughts interrupted by the sound of an approaching siren, and relief flowed through her as the ambulance arrived. Charlie moved the first-aid kit out of the way, then showed the paramedics the best way down the rocks. Jess recognised both men, who greeted her by name, their surprise evident as she debriefed them and they realised the role she had played in events.

Things passed in a blur after that. Charlie left, but Jess remained where she was, answering the occasional question but mostly watching the paramedics work. It wasn't long before they were joined by the medics from the air ambulance and she had to give her debrief over again. Once the boy was stabilised, volunteers were needed to help extricate the stretcher from the difficult location, but before long he was off the rocks and on his way to St Piran's in the helicopter.

'Now, then, Jess, our heroine of the day, what about you?' Stuart asked, squatting down in front of her while Mark cleared up their things and invited the more nosy and persistent onlookers to disperse.

'Me?' Jess frowned. 'I'm fine.'

He chuckled. 'I hardly think so, love. You're pale as a ghost and your leg is a mess,' he pointed out.

'I'd forgotten all about it,' she admitted, so focused had she been on what she needed to do.

'You were a bit busy, weren't you?' His grin was infectious. 'Are you hurt anywhere else?'

'Just some cuts and bruises. I bashed my side and twisted my foot when I fell. It's nothing. I'll clean up at home,' she assured him, anxiety setting in at the prospect of either Stuart or Mark treating her.

Pulling on a fresh pair of protective gloves, Stuart sat back and looked at her. 'That's a deep cut, Jess. You've lost a fair bit of blood and it's going to need stitching. And that's without getting the other things checked out.'

Her anxiety increasing, Jess bit her lip. She wished she could dismiss her injuries and refuse treatment, but looking at her leg she could see that the wound was bad and not something she would advise anyone else to try and take care of alone. As the adrenalin that had sustained her while waiting for the ambulance wore off, her foot and her ribs were also becoming increasingly painful and she feared she might have broken at least one bone. All of which meant she was going to have to tell Stuart the truth.

Fighting back an uncharacteristic welling up

of tears, she sucked in a ragged breath. 'Stuart, I…' She hesitated, frightened what would happen when he knew.

'What's wrong, Jess?' he prompted, his concern evident.

'You need to double-glove,' she told him, her voice unsteady, her lashes lowering so that she wouldn't see the expression on his face. 'I'm HIV positive.'

A few seconds of silence followed and she felt sick as she waited for the inevitable reaction to her admission. An errant tear escaped and landed on her cheek. It was Stuart's hand that reached out to wipe it away and she glanced up, wide-eyed with surprise to see nothing but understanding and compassion in the forty-year-old father-of-three's hazel eyes.

'Don't you worry, Jess, love. We'll take good care of you.'

His kindness and easy acceptance, so at odds with her earlier experiences—apart from Gio, of course—brought a fresh welling up of emotion. As Stuart set about dressing her leg, Jess struggled to push thoughts of Gio to the back of her mind. She wished more than anything that he was there with her now. But he wasn't. She was on her own. Just as she had been these last four years.

Before she knew it, they were setting off on the thirty-minute drive from Penhally to St Piran, arriving a long time after the air ambulance had deposited their casualty. Stuart and Mark were wonderful, as was Ben Carter, into whose experienced, caring and understanding hands they delivered her.

Supportive and reassuring, Ben guarded her confidentiality and refused to make an issue of her status. By the time she had been X-rayed— thankfully there proved to be no breaks—and returned to A and E to have the deep cut on her leg stitched, her other cuts and grazes cleaned and a supportive bandage put on her swollen, painful foot, she was feeling tired and woozy. The antibiotics and pain medication she'd been given didn't help.

Dismissing the nurse who had waited with her, Ben drew up a chair, sat down and sent her a warm smile. 'I know you wanted news. The boy's name is Will. He's in Theatre and has the best of chances, thanks to you. You saved his life today, Jess. Care to tell me how you did it?' he asked, signing off her notes and closing the file.

Her defences lowered by all that had happened, not just with Will and her own injury but the deep pain of Gio's rejection and withdrawal, she found herself pouring the whole story out to Ben.

'Surgery's loss is St Piran's gain,' he told her a while later when her flow of words had ended.

'Thank you.'

'Does Gio know? Do you want me to call him?'

The two questions brought a fresh threat of tears. 'Yes, he knows,' she admitted, trying to steady her voice before she continued, forcing out the words. 'But don't call him. He's in Italy. And we're just friends.'

'Friends?' Ben raised a sceptical eyebrow.

'You heard about his wife?' she asked. When Ben nodded, she continued. 'He's not ready for a new relationship. Even if he was, it's too much for him to take on someone like me.'

'I wouldn't give up on him too quickly, Jess.'

She appreciated Ben's kindness but she had little hope left in fairy-tales. Resting her head back, feeling very tired, she sighed. 'Can I go home?'

'Not for a while, especially as you'll be on your own once you get there,' he added brushing aside her half-hearted protest.

A knock on the door curbed further conversation and senior staff nurse Ellen came in. Although she smiled, it was clear that something was bothering her and, before she closed the door, Jess heard the sound of some sort of commotion going on somewhere in the department.

'I'm sorry to interrupt,' Ellen apologised. 'Ben, we have a problem out here. Can you come?'

'Yes, of course. Rest here for a while and try not to worry about anything, Jess. I'll be back shortly to see you,' he promised, giving her hand a squeeze before pushing back the chair and rising to his feet.

'Thanks, Ben.'

'Is there anything I can get for you, love?' Ellen asked, taking a moment to fuss with the sheet and pillows and make sure she was comfortable.

Feeling tired and washed out, Jess managed a smile. 'No, thanks. I'm fine.'

As they left the room, leaving her alone, Jess closed her eyes. It was one thing to tell her not to worry, but she was finding it impossible when her thoughts were fixed firmly on Gio. Despite thinking she could never trust a man again, in such a short time she had fallen irrevocably in love. But he couldn't feel the same about her and now, when she most needed his arms around her, he wasn't there. Ben had told her not to give up, but why would Gio want someone who was living with a condition that could change at any moment and drastically reduce her life expectancy, causing him to lose someone else?

She'd taken a huge risk, opening her heart and allowing Gio into her life, and all too briefly she'd experienced a piece of heaven before it had been ripped away from her again. She had no idea what the future held in store. After years of uncertainty, she had found a place where she felt at home and could settle. Was that now all to change because of Gio?

As much as he'd enjoyed his couple of days back home in Italy, and especially celebrating his parents' fortieth wedding anniversary, Gio continued to feel edgy and unsettled. For once it was nothing to do with returning to a place that reminded him of Sofia. His disquiet was all due to Jessica. Within hours he would be flying back to the UK and driving to the house he had shared with her in St Piran these last weeks. Knowing that she wouldn't be there made that return a dismal prospect.

'Something is troubling you, *figlio*.'

Gio looked up as his father joined him on the terrace and he gave a wry smile, unsurprised by the older man's insight. 'I'm fine, *Papà*.'

'Tell me about his woman.'

'What woman?' Gio prevaricated, shifting uncomfortably.

'You said you might be bringing a friend this weekend,' he reminded, 'but you came alone.'

'I might have meant a male friend.'

His father chuckled. 'You might. But you didn't. My guess is that you were referring to the woman who has been staying with you. The woman responsible for bringing you back to life these last weeks, bringing laughter and happiness back to your eyes.'

Gio sighed, somewhat stunned by his father's words. And by the realisation, the truth, of how much Jessica had changed him in the short time he had known her. He leaned against the railing and gazed out at the familiar Piedmont country-side. It was home—and yet now his heart felt as if it belonged elsewhere.

'Gio?'

Turning round, he pulled up a chair next to his father. 'I think I've made a big mistake, *Papà*.'

It had not been his intention to unburden himself, but now he found himself telling his father all about Jessica—and his dilemma.

'*Figlio*, you have never lacked courage. Do not start doubting yourself and your feelings now,' his father advised when he had finally run out of words.

'What do you mean?' Gio asked with a

frown, running the fingers of one hand through his hair.

'Tell me,' his father asked, leaning forward and resting his elbows on his knees, his gaze direct, 'would you have forgone the life you had with Sofia if you had known in advance that you would lose her when you did?'

A flash of anger flared within him at the question. 'Of course not!'

'That is what I thought.' His father smiled and although his tone gentled, his words lost none of their impact. 'Yet now you risk throwing away this second chance for love and happiness because you fear that you will one day lose Jessica, too.'

'*Papà…*'

His father gestured with one hand to silence him. 'Jessica is clearly a very special woman and she has become very important to you. You love her, I can see it in your eyes and hear it in your voice when you speak of her, and yet you're holding back. I know the pain and heartache you suffered when Sofia died. We all miss her. What you had together was so rare and so special. Few of us are blessed with that kind of happiness *once* in a lifetime, let alone *twice*,' the older man pointed out with a shake of his head.

In the brief pause that followed, the words sank in and Gio reflected on just how lucky he had been. He looked up as his father rested a hand on his shoulder and continued.

'We are all going to die at some time. What is important is what we do with the time we have. You have made us so proud, *figlio*, not only with your career and the work you do in Sofia's name but also because of the person you are. From all you have told me of her, your Jessica is a rare woman, and not one who would ever now trust herself to a man lightly. Yet she has trusted herself to *you*. Are you going to let her down? Are you going to let fear turn you away from love and the many years you could have together?'

The questions hit him full force, shocking him, but his father had not yet finished with him.

'Sofia would be so angry with you, Gio. She wanted you to live, to be happy, to love. Now you have found someone worthy of you, someone who has brought so much to your life. Don't throw that away, *figlio,*' he pleaded softly. 'You have our blessing, and Ginetta's, too,' he added, referring to Sofia's mother, who remained part of their family. 'You deserve new love and happiness. So does Jessica. Follow your heart…go back to the place that has become your home and show the woman who has given you so much the kind of man I know you to be.'

Hours later everything his father said still resonated in his head. It was early on Monday morning but he had given up trying to sleep. He had driven past Jessica's cottage before coming home from the airport but her car had not been there and it was clear no one was in. When he had also been unable to reach her by phone, unease had set in. Where was she?

Now he stared out of the window, seeing nothing but the darkness. There was also darkness inside himself. The house had felt cold and stark and lonely without Jessica, as he had feared it would. And so had he. All the joy and fun and warmth had left it with her departure. A departure he could blame on no one but himself.

He pressed one palm to the hollow ache in

his chest. He had been so blind, so stupid. How could he have ever believed that he could live for the rest of his life in a vacuum? He hadn't been living at all, only existing. It was Jessica who had brought meaning back to his world again and had made him want to embrace life in every way.

Leaning his forehead against the coolness of the glass, he reflected on his mistakes. He had coaxed and cajoled Jessica into trusting him, caring for him, opening up to him. He'd taken what she had given him without properly considering just what it must have taken for her to trust, and exactly what that trust meant. She had shown such courage, while he had got cold feet. In doing so he had behaved as abominably as her ex-fiancé, her family and her former friends and colleagues had. How must Jessica be feeling now? *He* felt lower than low when he forced himself to consider what his withdrawal, his insistence that they could have nothing but friendship, must have done to her.

Dio!

How was he going to put things right?

Because he could see now with startling clarity

that all his father had said was true. And he thought of Luca, who had been through a similar kind of loss as his own and who'd had the courage to let love back into his life again. He was a doctor, Gio chided himself. He knew that Jessica could fall ill tomorrow—but equally she could live a long and normal lifespan, keeping fit and well. Given the right care and precautions, even having a healthy child free of HIV was not the impossibility she believed it to be. Whatever she wished, he would support her all the way.

No one knew what the future held in store, just as his father and Luca had said. And facing the rest of his life alone was no longer the answer he had once thought. He could not guard himself from hurt without denying himself all the joys. And he knew now, after such a short time without Jessica, that he didn't want to waste any more time alone. Whether they had five years or fifty years, he wanted to share every moment with her. If she would forgive him and allow him a second chance.

Jessica had trusted him in the most elemental way and he had let her down. The knowledge cut him to the quick. In the face of her bravery he had been nothing but a coward. Were he to be lucky enough to win her back, he would spend the rest of their lives together proving to her that she was loved and cherished. Going downstairs, he made coffee and stepped outside into the coolness of the pre-dawn air, lost in his thoughts.

Along with the album Sofia had made of their lives had been a final letter for him. He carried it with him always, with her photo, next to his heart. He knew it word for word as she told him how much she loved him, that every moment had been worth it because they had been together, how she respected him and supported him.

'You must go on with your career, Cori, and with your life. Grieve for me, but not for too long. We have been so blessed and had so much more in twenty-two years than many people have in a whole lifetime. I know you, *amore mio*. And I beg you to move on, not to stay alone and sad for the rest of your life. I want you to be happy, fulfilled, cared for. You have so much love to give. Open your heart, Cori. For me. I will always be with you and will always love you. Look up at the night sky and the brightest star will be me smiling down on you, wishing you the best of everything and for a special woman to love you as I love you.'

His throat tight with emotion, he turned his gaze up to the sky, finding the brightest star. He thought of Sofia's words, of her wish for him, her blessing, and realised he was letting her down by refusing to accept all life had to offer him. Had their places been reversed, he would have wanted the same for her...that she would find someone to care for her, who would make her happy. And his courageous, spirited Sofia would grieve, would never forget, but would face life with her customary bravery. Just as Jessica was doing in her own way, making a whole new life for herself after being so badly betrayed and left to cope with the devastation alone. He owed it to Sofia, to Jessica and to himself to step back into life.

He looked back at the star, opening his heart, knowing Sofia would always be there, that he would never forget and would always love her, but that there was room and a special place for

Jessica, too. It was time. For a moment it seemed as if the star glowed even brighter, filling him with a sense of peace. As dawn broke, the stars fading as the sky slowly lightened, bringing a rosy glow to the magnificent Cornish coastline, Gio knew what he had to do.

CHAPTER ELEVEN

'OH, MY God.' Jess felt her whole world shattering into tiny pieces as she stared in horrified disbelief at the local newspaper. This couldn't be happening. 'How? Why?'

Ben sat solemn-faced beside her, appearing tired and drawn, as if he hadn't slept in the hours since she'd last seen him. 'I'm sorry, Jess. We tried to stop it.'

Fighting back tears and a terrible sense of doom, she re-examined the lurid headline emblazoned in large letters across the front page…

HOSPITAL HEROINE HAS HIV!

The night was a blur. She'd fallen asleep in A and E, knocked out by the medication and emotional exhaustion. 'We don't normally have staff sleeping in the department overnight but we made an exception for you,' Josh had teased her when he'd checked her over before the night shift ended.

When Ben had come back on duty, she'd discovered that the disturbance he'd been called to had been caused by Kennie Vernon, a reporter on the *St Piran Gazette*, known as 'Vermin' for his unpleasant methods and his motto of never allowing the truth to spoil a good story. She'd met him once when he'd delved unsuccessfully into the background of a patient in her care, and he'd left an unfavourable impression. Short and stout, his greasy black hair worn in a narrow ponytail, he had a goatee beard, beady brown eyes and a shifty nature.

'One of the bystanders in Penhally overheard you telling the paramedics about the HIV and informed Kennie. The bastard ran with that angle of the story.' Ben's anger and disgust were evident. 'He came poking around A and E. I threw him out. You were sleeping, so Josh and I decided to keep you here. We didn't want you going home alone or risk you running into Kennie.'

Jess wrapped her arms around herself, unable to stop shaking. 'What am I going to do?'

'You told me about the appalling way you were treated when you were first diagnosed, but that isn't going to happen here,' he reassured her, but she lacked belief.

'Right.'

Ben took her hand. 'You'll be surprised, Jess. I'm not, because I know you are loved and respected. There may be one or two idiots, but ninety-nine percent of the hospital are supporting you. We've had endless calls sending you good wishes and they're continuing to come in.'

Jess didn't know what to say.

'We took the liberty of making some arrangements on your behalf,' he continued, and nervousness fluttered in her stomach.

'What arrangements?'

'Flora wanted to help. She said she held a spare key for your cottage in case of an emergency?' Jess nodded, trying to take everything in. 'Knowing you'd worry, she's picked up your kittens and will look after them for as long as you need.'

'Thank you,' she murmured, surprised but relieved.

'Your car remains where you left it in Penhally, so you'll need a lift to pick it up, but Megan met Flora at your cottage and collected some things you might need.'

Fresh tears pricked her eyes. For someone who seldom cried, she could have filled a swimming pool this last week. She didn't ask, but the person she most wanted to know about, and to see, was Gio. He'd be back from Italy. He might even be in the hospital, she realised, glancing at her watch, shocked by the time. What would he think? She felt sick with worry.

When Ben left, Jess gingerly slipped out of bed, thankful for the adjacent shower room that meant she didn't have to wander down the corridor in the unflattering hospital gown she was wearing. After a wash, she sat on the bed, feeling emotionally and physically battered as she wondered what to do.

'Where is she?'

Jess heard Megan's anxious question from outside and someone's voice mumble in reply.

She barely had a moment to compose herself before her friend rushed in, her face pale and tears spiking her eyelashes. Without uttering a word, Megan dropped a carrier bag on the bed and wrapped her in a hug.

'You silly, silly girl,' she admonished, halfway between a laugh and a sob. 'Oh, how I wish I'd known. I can't bear to think of you going through this alone.'

Megan's acceptance and support was overwhelming. Jess began to explain, her voice shaky and whisper soft, when Brianna arrived. She looked as worried and upset as Megan. And, like Megan, Brianna's first instinct was to hug her.

With her friends giving the caring support she had never expected to know, Jess told them what she had told Gio—about Duncan, her diagnosis, the prejudice, ignorance and discrimination she'd encountered, and being disowned by her family. They were all crying by the time she had finished.

'I'd have been scared witless doing an emergency cricothyroidotomy,' Megan admitted when the talk moved on to the incident on the rocks and Jess's former career. 'I'm in awe at what you did.'

Brianna hugged her again. 'We all are. You're amazing, Jess. How far through your training were you?'

'I'd qualified and had begun a trauma rotation when I was diagnosed. I wanted to be a surgeon but was advised to find another career.'

'That's awful,' Brianna stated.

'It is,' Megan agreed. 'But it explains why you're so knowledgeable and able to explain things to patients when we don't have time. Do you miss it?'

'At first I was devastated. I attended an HIV support group and someone there suggested I think about counselling,' she told them, sharing things she'd told no one but Gio. 'I could continue helping people but without physical contact. I enjoy what I do and wouldn't change it now.'

'What about Gio?' Megan asked softly.

'He wants friendship, that's all.' It didn't become any easier with repetition. 'I understand why after he lost his wife. And it isn't as if I have anything to offer him.'

'Stuff and nonsense!' Brianna exclaimed, her Irish accent stronger than usual.

It hurt too much to talk about Gio so Jess changed the subject and reflected on the damage the newspaper article might have caused. The nightmare was real, the secret she had guarded was now public knowledge, and she feared the consequences. She was mulling over what to do when Ben returned.

'I'd rather you had a couple of days off and rested that leg, but sitting at home alone won't be good for you.' He frowned, deep in thought. 'We can look out for you here at the hospital. Just be sensible and don't over-stretch your side. And keep your foot up as much as possible. I've brought you some pain medication. Come and see us if you're not feeling well or you have problems with the wound.'

Jess took the tablets and smiled. 'OK. Thanks, Ben, you've been wonderful. How's Lucy?'

'About to pop!' he said, making them laugh.

'She's fed up and excited. We can't wait for the baby to arrive.'

Jess noticed Megan's and Brianna's smiles dimmed and both had pain in their eyes. She suspected her friends carried secrets and had been hurt in the past, and she wished there was something she could do to help them.

After Ben had given her a hug and final instructions, he returned to work. Megan and Brianna had to do the same but, before leaving, they arranged to meet up for lunch. Before heading to her office and what could be an uncomfortable chat with her boss, Jess changed into the clothes Megan had collected for her and went up to the ward to check on Will, anxious to know how he was. She felt nervous and unsure of the reception she would receive from colleagues and patients.

Driving to the hospital, Gio joined the queue at the traffic lights, his gaze straying to the pavement outside the newsagent's shop. His heart threatened to stop as he noted the headline on the local paper. Pasted onto a sandwich board for all to see, it shrieked out at him…

HOSPITAL HEROINE HAS HIV!

He swore furiously in Italian. There was little doubt to whom the headline referred. What the hell had been going on while he'd been in Italy? Anxious for Jessica and desperate to find out what lay behind the headline, he waited in frustration as the lights changed and the traffic moved forward then made his way as fast as he could to the hospital.

Dread clutched at him as he parked his car and hurried inside. One of the first people he saw was Ben, who gave him a brief résumé of events and then showed him the newspaper. While he felt deep concern for her well-being and fury at the thoughtless reporter, he was also full of pride at the way Jessica had saved the young man's life.

'Thank you for taking such good care of her,' he said now, shaking Ben's hand. 'Where is she?'

'She left here about five minutes ago and was

going to visit Will in Intensive Care before going to her office.'

'Thanks,' he repeated.

Ben nodded, holding his gaze. 'Jess needs you, Gio,' his friend told him, and he knew he deserved the hint of chastisement that had laced the words.

'I need her, too,' he confided, earning himself a smile. 'I won't let her down again.'

Determined, he set off to find her.

'May I sit down?' Josh asked, taking advantage of the rare opportunity of finding Megan sitting alone in the canteen.

'OK.'

The agreement was grudging, but at least she *had* agreed and hadn't told him to go away. He set down his mug of coffee and pulled up a chair.

She looked at him, a small frown on her face. 'You look tired.'

'Is that a polite way of saying rough?' he teased with a wry smile, running the palm of one hand across his stubbled jaw, intrigued by the flush that brought a wash of colour to her pale cheeks.

'No, I didn't mean that.'

'I've just pulled an extra couple of night shifts and needed the caffeine fix before going home for some sleep. I'm back on days tomorrow,' he explained, savouring the hot, reviving drink.

What he didn't tell her was that he'd been doing extra shifts to avoid having to go home. Things were becoming more and more untenable with Rebecca and he didn't know what to do about it. They had grown further apart than ever. He had tried to encourage her to get out of the house, to take up some kind of voluntary work or hobby if she didn't want to get a job. Anything to give her something else to focus on instead of sitting at home working out ways to try and persuade him to change his mind about having a baby.

He wasn't going to change his mind. Ever. What he hadn't told Rebecca was that he had once teetered on the brink of fatherhood—unknowingly and no more willingly as that may have been at the time. He took another drink, his gaze fixed on Megan. Since talking to her and hearing once and for all that her baby had been his, he'd been able to think of little else.

Hearing in words the reality that he had held his tiny, lifeless son in his hands had hit him far harder than he had ever expected. And it had only made him more certain that having a baby with Rebecca was the wrong thing to do in so many ways, for him, for her and, most importantly of all, for any resulting child.

Setting down his mug, he folded his arms and leaned on the table, watching as Megan spread honey on a granary roll. 'How's Jess?'

'A bit sore. Very upset about the newspaper report. That beastly man,' she growled, echoing his feelings and those of everyone he knew.

'Poor Jess. No one needs that kind of thing.' He shook his head. 'I think people are more stunned at discovering she's a qualified doctor and saved that boy's life than anything else.'

Megan licked sticky honey off her finger, a simple gesture but one that nearly stopped his heart and brought a wave of all-too-familiar desire—the same desire he had always felt for her and her alone.

'Megan...'

'Don't, Josh, please. I—' Her words snapped off, her expression changing as she looked beyond him. He sensed her complete withdrawal, but before he could ask what was wrong, she spoke again. 'Your wife is here.'

He swore under his breath, looking round and seeing Rebecca standing just inside the entrance of the canteen. As always she looked picture perfect. Expensively dressed, polished, outwardly beautiful...and completely out of place.

'Megan,' he began again, returning his attention to her, not at all sure what he wanted to say, still so confused and churned up inside, knowing only that he resented Rebecca's intrusion.

'Just go, Josh.'

After a moment of indecision he rose to his feet, spurred into action as Rebecca spotted him and began to close the distance between them. After an inadequate word of farewell, he left Megan and worked his way between the tables towards Rebecca and the exit.

'What are you doing here?' he asked, taking her arm to steer her out of the canteen, irritation

shooting through him, compounded by the tiredness of two long night shifts.

She made her customary pout. 'You said the
garage wouldn't have your car ready until this
afternoon, so I thought I'd surprise you and pick
you up.'

'I told you there was no need.'

They walked in silence towards the exit. A
silence that spoke volumes about the physical,
mental and emotional distance between them.
They had nothing to speak about, nothing left
in common. They didn't talk any more. He wondered if they ever had. One thing was certain…
he could never share with her the jumble of emotions that continued to rage within him about
Megan and about Stephen, their lost son.

'You! Ms Carmichael. Or Dr Carmichael…what-
ever your name is!'

Leaving Intensive Care after visiting Will, who
was making good progress, and having been
thanked by his grateful parents who had seen
the newspaper report but were just relieved that
their son was alive, Jess halted. Her stomach

churned as she turned to face the man whose angry voice had bellowed her name.

She'd been overwhelmed by the support she'd received from colleagues, many of whom had made a point of stopping her on her walk from A and E to Intensive Care. Now she was forced to encounter someone who sounded far from friendly.

The man was short and stocky with a ruddy complexion and a receding hairline. His heavy footsteps pounded on the floor as he strode determinedly towards her. Nervous, Jess heard the familiar ping that announced the arrival of one of the lifts, accompanied by the soft whooshing sound as the door opened. Unfortunately the lift was too far away for her to use it as an escape route.

'It's outrageous that you are allowed to walk around this hospital so close to vulnerable patients,' the man stated loudly, making her cringe with embarrassment. 'I don't want you anywhere near my wife.'

As the man continued his tirade, his language becoming ever more abusive, Jess was very aware that they were drawing a crowd. People walking the corridors stopped to see what was going on, while others emerged from nearby wards and offices. No one intervened. She was on her own.

Alarmed and humiliated, Jess stepped back, only to find her path blocked as she came up against something solid and strong and warm. Before she could even draw breath and absorb the fact that Gio was really here, one of his arms wrapped around her, across the front of her shoulders, drawing her against his familiar frame, making her feel protected.

'That is enough, sir.' Gio didn't raise his voice and yet his words rang with such authority and steely command that her detractor at once fell silent. 'You have no business abusing any member of hospital staff at any time, and even less so when your information is wrong and you are speaking from ignorance.'

'But—'

'But nothing. Jessica is a highly valued and respected colleague. Her status is no one's business but her own and she poses absolutely no danger to anyone else,' he stated firmly, his hold on her tightening as she relaxed into him, drawing on his strength. 'Yesterday she saved the life of a young man who would have died had she not been there. For her courage and her selflessness she deserves gratitude and praise, not the ill-informed comments and judgemental attitudes of people who do not know what they are talking about.'

Jess remained speechless with amazement as Gio launched into his defence of her, declaring his support of and belief in her. But even when the man who had challenged her had been si-lenced and walked away by Security, she discov-ered that Gio had more to say, uncaring of their audience of colleagues, patients and visitors who remained.

'I am so proud of you, Jessica, and so sorry that I was not here for you when you needed me,' he declared, gently turning her round and cupping her face in his hands. She stared into intense blue eyes, every part of her shaking. 'I love you. I want to marry you and spend the rest of my life with you…if you will have me and forgive me for being so stupid this week and letting you down.'

Jess barely heard the gasps of delight and whispered comments from the people around them. All she could see, all she could hear, all she cared about was Gio, the man who had changed her life in such a short time, who believed in her and accepted her and who had just announced his love for her to the world.

'If I'll have you?'

She didn't know whether to laugh or to cry! So she did both. At the same time. He was everything she wanted. All she wanted. After the last few days of pain and uncertainty, thinking she could never have more than his friendship, she could hardly dare to believe this was true. For now, a wave of love and joy swamped the doubts that still lingered within her. Uncaring of where they were, of her painful side and throbbing leg—even of providing more gossip fodder for nosy Rita—she wrapped her arms around his neck, welcoming the instant response as his own arms enclosed her and held her close.

'I love you, too,' she managed through her tears.

As he swept her off her feet and into a passionate kiss, she dimly heard the whistles and whoops, the calls of congratulations and the spontaneous round of applause. She kissed him back with equal fervour and with all the emotion, love and thankfulness that swelled her heart.

After what had seemed the longest of days, and when he finally had Jessica to himself, Gio could not banish the flicker of unease that nagged at him. Concerned for her well-being and her injuries, he had brought her home to her cottage and insisted she rest while he cooked them a meal. She had eaten it, but she had grown quieter and quieter as the evening progressed. Now, as she paced the living room, her limp evident, he could bear the suspense no more.

As she passed within reach of his armchair, he caught her hand and drew her down to sit on his lap. A deep sigh escaped her and although she didn't pull away from him, she was far from relaxed.

'What is wrong, *fiamma*?' he asked, scared that she was having doubts and changing her mind. 'You are so restless. Talk to me.'

'I can't thank you enough for what you did today. It was horrible and I didn't know what to do.' For a moment she hesitated, her gaze averted, then she sighed again and looked at him, revealing the shadows in her olive-green eyes. 'Then you were there and made everything right.'

So why did he suddenly feel that things were now wrong? His heart lurched in fear. 'Jessica...'

'I won't hold you to it. I'll understand if it was something you said on the spur of the moment because of the circumstances,' she told him in a rush, her voice shaky.

'You won't hold me to what?' he asked, genuinely puzzled.

Long lashes lowered to mask her expression and her voice dropped to a whisper. 'Marrying me. You don't have to.'

'You don't want me to?'

'Yes. No. Not if you don't want to.'

She frowned in confusion and he felt bad for

teasing her, but now he could see to the root of her worries, it felt as if a huge weight had lifted from his shoulders. He understood her doubts. He deserved them after the way he had behaved. But this, he hoped, he could deal with.

'Look at me.' He cupped her face with one hand, drawing her gaze to his. 'It is true I had not planned on asking you to marry me in such a way, with so many people listening. But at the time a public declaration seemed right.' Uncertainty remained in her eyes. 'Can you pass me my jacket?'

'OK.'

He held her steady as, her frown deepening, she reached out to retrieve the jacket of his suit, which he had discarded and left draped over the arm of the adjacent sofa.

'Thank you.' With his free hand he checked the pockets until he found what he needed. 'The timing and the setting may have been unplanned, but I meant every word I said.'

He heard her indrawn gasp of surprise and she looked at him with a mix of warring emotions in her eyes. 'Gio?'

'I'm not surprised you doubted me. I deserve that after the terrible way I behaved last week,' he told her, pressing a finger to her lips to silence her protests. 'It needs to be said, *fiamma*. I was wrong. I knew how badly other people had treated you and yet I allowed my own momentary fears to rise up and my withdrawal, timed with my trip to Italy, must have felt like another rejection of you. I am so sorry.'

'Don't.' She caught his hand, their fingers instinctively linking together. 'I understand. And I don't blame you.'

'You should.'

She shook her head, her loose hair shimmering and dancing like living fire. 'No. You went through so much with Sofia. I knew you were scared of going through anything like that again. And, let's face it, the odds could be less good with me.'

'I do not care about odds, Jessica, I care about *you*,' he insisted. 'I never imagined that I could fall in love again, that I would ever know happiness and peace again, but my life changed for the better the moment I met you. Thanks to you I stopped existing and started living again.'

'Gio,' she whispered, her eyes bright with unshed tears.

'Please, I need to say this.' He drew her hand to his mouth and kissed it. 'I hate that I hurt you, that my withdrawal left you so lonely and uncertain. You deserved so much more from me and, if you will let me, I'll spend the rest of our lives proving to you how much I love you and that I'll never let you down again.' He paused a moment, sucking in an unsteady breath, his heart thudding against his ribs. 'I came back from Italy knowing what an idiot I had been and knowing what I wanted and needed to do. Events overtook us, and my plans went awry.'

Eyes wide with disbelief and hope, she bit her lip, her fingers clinging to his. 'What plans?' she managed, and he could feel the tremble running through her.

'My plans to be with you alone, like this, to beg your forgiveness and to ask you properly to be my wife.' Holding her gaze, he released her hand and reached into his pocket once more, drawing out the box. 'I bought this in Italy. For you. I meant all I said this morning, I just meant to say it in private! So the timing may have been wrong, but the question was heartfelt and genuine, not something I made up on the spot.' He placed the little box in her hand. 'Jessica, I love you. I want to spend the rest of my life cherishing you, being your friend and your lover. Please, will you make me the happiest and luckiest of men and marry me?'

'Yes. Yes, yes, yes!'

Jess felt as if her heart had swollen so full of love and joy that it would surely stop beating. All day doubts had nagged at her, but now her fears had been allayed as Gio had laid his own heart on the line for her. Again. Her vision blurred by tears, her fingers shaking so badly she could hardly make them work properly, she did as he encouraged and opened the jeweller's box.

'Oh, my,' she gasped. 'Gio!'

'You like it?' he asked nervously, and she laughed through her tears that he could doubt it.

She gazed down at the gorgeous ring. Set in

platinum were three stunning olive apatite stones that exactly matched those in the earrings her grandmother had given her and which she wore every day. The three stones were set on a slight angle with the shoulders of the ring overlapping each side, each sparkling with a row of tiny diamonds. It was the most divine ring she had ever seen. She didn't dare imagine how much it had cost but it was not the monetary value that mattered, it was that Gio had chosen something so special, with such care, knowing what it would mean to her and giving it to her with love.

'It's beautiful,' she murmured huskily as he took it from the box and set it on her finger. 'Perfect. Thank you.'

'You are perfect and beautiful.'

He cupped her face, bestowing on her the gentlest and most exquisite of kisses. Jess sank into him, wrapping her arms around him, wondering how she had ever been lucky enough to know such happiness. As the passion flared between them, healing the past, uniting them heart and soul and full of promise for the future, she gave thanks for this very special man.

'I love your home,' Gio told her softly as they lay in bed later that night, replete after the physical expression of their love and togetherness. 'I feel at peace here,' he continued, filling her already overflowing heart with new joy as his feelings mirrored her own. 'Any day the fences will be ready and our menagerie will come home.'

'I thought maybe you'd arranged for that to be done so I'd leave your house and move back here,' she admitted softly.

'No!' He sounded so shocked she couldn't help but laugh, secure now in his feelings and her own. 'That was not why at all,' he insisted. 'It was to make you happy but also, selfishly, because I wanted to come here and to care for the animals with you. Can this *be* our home, *fiamma*? Can we bring this beautiful shell back to life together and make it ours for ever?'

'Yes, please!'

Snuggling into his embrace, she smiled into the darkness, knowing that they shared the same vision, not just for this place that would be their home but for their future. However long they were blessed with they would share together. And with the friends and colleagues who had shown them so much support and understanding.

It was not just the cottage that had been a shell that would be brought back to life. She and Gio had been shells, too. They had each been alone, rocked and ravaged by the events that had turned their lives upside down. But fate had brought them together…two people who had needed each other so much. They had found their place. Had found each other. And together they had found the sunshine, new hope and a fresh joy of living.

Safe in Gio's arms, Jess felt truly at peace, secure in a love, a friendship and a happiness that neither of them had ever expected to know again. They had been granted second chances and they had found their rightful place in this special part of Cornwall.

It had been a difficult journey but, finally, she was where she was meant to be…with Gio.

MEDICAL™

Large Print

Titles for the next six months...

August

CEDAR BLUFF'S MOST ELIGIBLE BACHELOR	Laura Iding
DOCTOR: DIAMOND IN THE ROUGH	Lucy Clark
BECOMING DR BELLINI'S BRIDE	Joanna Neil
MIDWIFE, MOTHER...ITALIAN'S WIFE	Fiona McArthur
ST PIRAN'S: DAREDEVIL, DOCTOR...DAD!	Anne Fraser
SINGLE DAD'S TRIPLE TROUBLE	Fiona Lowe

September

SUMMER SEASIDE WEDDING	Abigail Gordon
REUNITED: A MIRACLE MARRIAGE	Judy Campbell
THE MAN WITH THE LOCKED AWAY HEART	Melanie Milburne
SOCIALITE...OR NURSE IN A MILLION?	Molly Evans
ST PIRAN'S: THE BROODING HEART SURGEON	Alison Roberts
PLAYBOY DOCTOR TO DOTING DAD	Sue MacKay

October

TAMING DR TEMPEST	Meredith Webber
THE DOCTOR AND THE DEBUTANTE	Anne Fraser
THE HONOURABLE MAVERICK	Alison Roberts
THE UNSUNG HERO	Alison Roberts
ST PIRAN'S: THE FIREMAN AND NURSE LOVEDAY	Kate Hardy
FROM BROODING BOSS TO ADORING DAD	Dianne Drake

MEDICAL™

Large Print

Discover Pure Reading Pleasure with

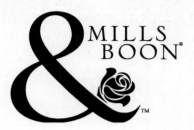

Visit the Mills & Boon website for all the latest in romance

- **Buy** all the latest releases, backlist and eBooks

- **Join** our community and chat to authors and other readers

- **Win** with our fantastic online competitions

- **Tell us** what you think by signing up to our reader panel

- **Find out** more about our authors and their books

- **Free** online reads from your favourite authors

- **Sign** up for our free monthly eNewsletter

- **Rate** and review books with our star system

www.millsandboon.co.uk

 Follow us at twitter.com/millsandboonuk

 Become a fan at facebook.com/romancehq